TALES OF THUBWAY THAM

TALES OF
THUBWAY THAM

JOHNSTON McCULLEY

WILDSIDE PRESS

TALES OF THUBWAY THAM

"Thubway Tham's Inthane Moment" originally appeared in *Detective Story Magazine*, Nov. 19. 1918. "Thubway Tham's Thanksgiving Dinner originally appeared in *Detective Story Magazine*, Nov. 26, 1918. "Thubway Tham's Understudy" originally appeared in *Detective Story Magazine*, Dec. 31, 1918. "Thubway Tham's Baggage Check" originally appeared in *Detective Story Magazine*, March 15, 1919. "Thubway Tham, Philanthropist" originally appeared in *Detective Story Magazine*, April 1, 1919. "Thubway Tham's Chrithtmath" originally appeared in *Detective Story Magazine*. "Thubway Tham's Glorious Fourth" originally appeared in *Detective Story Magazine*, Nov. 8, 1919. "Thubway Tham's Holdup" originally appeared in *Detective Story Magazine*, April 22, 1919. "Thubway Tham Meets Mr. Clackworthy" originally appeared in *Detective Story Magazine*, Feb 18, 1922. "Thubway Tham's Inthult" originally appeared in *Detective Story Magazine*, October 21, 1919.

CONTENTS

INTRODUCTION

JOHNSTON McCULLEY will be forever famous as the creator of Zorro, the Robin Hood-like hero of old California. But few realize how truly prolific and creative McCulley was throughout his long career as a writer.

McCulley (1883-1958) made the first true specialist pulp-fiction periodical, *Detective Story Magazine*, a special home for his work. In its pages he launched series after series . . . The Avenging Twins (who appeared in a series of eight adventures between 1923 and 1926), the Black Star (fourteen stories from 1916-1930), The Crimson Clown (seventeen stories from 1926-1931), The Man in Purple (three stories in 1921), The Spider (eleven stories between 1918 and 1919), Terry Trimble (four stories between 1917 and 1919), The Thunderbolt (three stories between 1920 and 1921) but most especially Thubway Tham (who appeared in more than one hundred and eighty stories between 1916 and 1948, at first in *Detective Story Magazine,* but later in such places as *Thrilling Detective*, with later reprints in *The Saint Mystery Magazine*, *Mike Shayne Mystery Magazine*, and others). The Thubway Tham series, you will note, starts before and lasts longer than all of McCulley's other mystery series combined! Clearly Tham was a favorite character, one to whom the author returned time and again.

Thubway Tham is a small, short-tempered gnome of a man, a professional pickpocket with an annoying lisp. But he is no mere thief . . . he is the king of his chosen profession, a master "dip" who works only in the subways of New York City. Like all such villains, he faces a cunning adversary in Police Detective Craddock, who is always half a pace behind. Craddock has sworn to put Tham behind bars, where he belongs. But Tham is clever enough to always remain one step ahead of Craddock and everyone else.

Despite being a criminal, Tham always comes off well: the people whom he relieves of their wallets are often deserving of it, and he has a tendency to take on other, much worse crooks to give them their just desserts. And, of course, there are scoundrels aplenty in his world: a rival pickpocket who moves in on his turf in "Thubway Tham's Baggage Check;" Shifty Shane, the holdup man, who calls Tham a coward because he doesn't use a gun; and Mr. Clackworthy, a slick grifter from Chicago[1], who looks down on dips as the lowest of thieves.

Call him an early antihero. Tham endears himself to readers because he has a moral compass. He knows his place is in the gutter of the world, but that doesn't mean he can't strive to better himself — or others.

If there is one theme running through these stories, it is that Tham is a thief with a heart of gold, even when it isn't always in his best interests. When he takes in a would-be apprentice in "Thubway Tham's Understudy," Tham knows very well that the boy may be his undoing. He does it anyway, and he nearly ends up in jail for his trouble. In "Thubway Tham's Insult," he takes offense at an actor's attitude toward thieves and decides to teach him a lesson. In "Thubway Tham's Baggage Check," he is disgusted by amateur thieves and plots to relieve them of their ill-gotten gains. Thieving should be left to professionals; amateurs are not permitted to dabble in Tham's trade. In "Thubway Tham, Philanthropist," Tham encounters an elderly couple living in squalor near his home and decides to help them, much to his eventual regret.

Tham also has time for charity on other holidays. On Thanksgiving, he gives a holiday dinner for nineteen newsies. On the Fourth of July, he takes time off to celebrate and gives advice to easy marks on how to protect their wallets and saves a lost little boy. On Christmas Eve, he sees an amateurish pickpocket steal a wallet on his beloved subway, so he steals in back and tries to return it to its rightful owner . . . with less than happy results. His heart really *is* in the right place.

So, give Tham a chance. Once you get beyond his lisp and gruff exte-

---

1   Mr. Amos Clackworthy, created by Christopher B. Booth, was the star of another long-running series in *Detective Story Magazine*; in a publicity stunt, McCulley and Booth each wrote a cross-over story involving both characters. In Booth's, Clackworthy gets the better of Thubway Tham. We present only McCulley's story here, however.

rior, you'll find a worthy and loyal friend. But keep an eye on your pockets; he's a master of his trade — as Mr. Clackworthy and so many others find out!

— John Gregory Betancourt
Holicong, Pennsylvania

THUBWAY THAM'S INTHANE MOMENT

DETECTIVE CRADDOCK stepped nearer the front of the little cigar store on the corner and almost pressed his nose against the window as he glanced inside. There was an expression of bewilderment on the countenance of the detective. His eyes bulged and then narrowed to two tiny slits as if he was considering something highly unusual and wondering just what it might mean. His lower jaw drooped and then came up again with a snap, expressing determination. To "get the goat" of Detective Craddock, who was a terror to those of the underworld, it was necessary only to attempt to "put something over" on him.

And Detective Craddock was not absolutely certain, of course, but he feared that a certain person was attempting to put something over on him now. And, to make matters worse, that certain person was no less a personage than Thubway Tham.

Thubway Tham was a clever pickpocket, one of the cleverest in the business, and he worked only in the subway during rush hours. He long ago had earned the name in the underworld of Subway Sam. And because, lisping, he called himself "Thubway Tham," everybody else did the same.

Some time since, Detective Craddock had resolved to "get" Thubway Tham. He had been honest enough to inform Tham of his determination, and between detective and dip there was a constant duel in which Craddock continually found himself the loser. Failure only whetted the appetite of the detective to take Thubway Tham in, however.

And now Detective Craddock looked through the window of the little cigar store, amazed. For Thubway Tham was inside and not purchasing a package of cigarettes or begging for a box of matches. Thubway Tham was behind the counter, waiting on trade.

Detective Craddock waited until there came a time when no customers were in the little shop, and then entered and stepped up to the counter. He grinned at Thubway Tham, but Tham's face expressed only the fact that he was a business man.

"What's the big idea?" Craddock wanted to know.

"I fail to grathp you," Thubway Tham told him.

"You do, eh? Try again. You grasp me, all right. What's the big idea of masquerading as an honest working man?"

"That *ith* what I am," Tham replied.

"Yes?"

"Yeth! And don't you come around here pethterin' me, either. I've got an honetht job, and I don't want to be bothered."

"There's something awfully fishy about this," Craddock said, "I haven't much faith in your reformation, Tham."

"No?"

"No! If it's a new game, Tham, old boy, I'll land you sooner or later."

"There you go! Justht becauthe once I wath thent up the river, you think I am alwayth goin' to be a crook! You don't give a man a chance, you copth!"

"No? Cut out the comedy, Tham. It doesn't impress me at all."

"The only way to impreth you would be with a brick againtht the bean!" Tham told him.

"Does your employer know you are a crook?"

"He knoth I wath once in prithon, if that ith what you mean." Tham said. "He thaid he wath ready to help a man get on the thraight path again."

"Very kind of him," Craddock commented.

"And if you pethter me, there'll be a howl! I'm thtraight, and you got to let me alone!"

Craddock purchased a cigar and stepped aside to light it as another customer entered. He stood back in a corner and watched Tham handle the customer. Presently he got the chance to speak to him once more.

"Go right ahead, Tham, old boy," he said. "But don't forget that I'll have an eye on you. This thing is a puzzle to me, but I'll work it out."

"I jutht dethided to be thraight," Tham complainingly told him. "I'm goin' to be honetht and work for my livin'. Every perthon hath an

11

inthane moment now and then. Maybe thith ith my inthane moment."

"There's sure something crazy about it," said Craddock.

The detective left the store, watched from the corner for a time, and then went about his business. He could not hope to catch Thubway Tham picking pockets while he was working behind the counter of a cigar store.

THAM GRINNED after Craddock had gone down the street and then gave his entire attention to the trade. It was the first day on duty, and he wanted to impress his boss, who would be coming in soon from the wholesale house. It might have been an insane moment, but Thubway Tham was enjoying it hugely, the more so because his actions mystified Detective Craddock.

He sold a package of cigarettes to an evil-looking youth and changed a five-dollar bill. Ten minutes later his employer, going through the cash register, found the bill and informed Thubway Tham that it was a counterfeit.

"Thtung!" Thubway Tham said. "I mutht be a thimp! I've got to thtand good for it, I thuppothe."

"You have," said his employer.

"I'll get thquare with that man, you can bet. I remember his fathe. I'll get him, all right!"

Thubway Tham was of a mind that it was a reflection on his cleverness to be stung like that. Were they playing him for an "easy mark" on his first day on the job, he wondered. He had agreed to work for fifteen dollars a week, and here was a third of his week's wages gone the first two hours on the job.

Thubway Tham put the counterfeit bill in his vest pocket and went about his business. During the noon hour he found little time to think of anything except selling cigars and tobacco. Then he went to luncheon, and was not pleased to discover that Detective Craddock was watching him closely.

Thubway Tham had an hour, and luncheon took but fifteen minutes. But he did not spend the other forty-five in the subway, "lifting a leather." He wandered around the streets, keeping away from subway entrances lest temptation prove too great, and at the appointed time returned to the cigar store and assumed his duties.

Detective Craddock, disgusted, went to another section of the city and sought to apprehend an evildoer.

There came a lull in business in the middle of the afternoon, and then it was that a well-dressed young man entered and announced his intention of purchasing a box of cigars that retailed at fifteen dollars the box.

Thubway Tham showed the goods eagerly, still determined to make an excellent record on his first day. He opened half a dozen boxes, that the prospective customer might select the particular color he desired. The telephone rang.

Tham hurried back to the instrument, which was at one end of the counter. It was his employer who called, and he gave minute instructions regarding a package of goods that should be wrapped up for a certain customer. Thubway Tham made a note with a pencil on a sheet of paper, hung up the receiver, and turned toward his customer again.

The customer was gone, and so were two boxes of the cigars, stock worth thirty dollars.

Thubway Tham gasped at the nerve of it. He realized that the man had had time to mingle in the crowd outside and get away. And the cigars, being of that special brand, would be missed. Unless the money was in the cash register for them, Thubway Tham's employer would think he had stolen them himself — for Tham remembered that the boss knew his past reputation.

Thubway Tham sighed and extracted thirty dollars from his own pocket and put the money in the till. He was getting wages of fifteen dollars a week, the first day of work was not done, and it had cost him thirty-five dollars altogether.

"It doth not pay to try to be honetht," Tham told himself. "A crook ith the motht honetht perthon in the world. I have been thtung again!"

He stored up anger against the man who had given him the counterfeit bill, and against the one who had stolen the cigars. Thubway Tham remembered faces well, and he promised to make those two men pay if ever he met them again.

The evening rush began, and Tham's, employer returned to aid him with the trade. For two hours Thubway Tham was kept busy continually, and then was told to go and get his dinner. He returned at the end of an hour, again successfully fighting away the temptation of the subway, and his boss went to get the evening meal.

There entered a man who filled Thubway Tham's heart with joy — until he remembered that he had turned honest.

"Ith thith your firtht vithit to New York?" Tham asked as he offered a box of cigars.

"How did you guess it?" the customer wanted to know.

"Oh, I jutht guethed it!" Tham replied.

"I'm here to see the sights."

"Yeth? You want to watch out for crookth."

Some sense of delicacy prevented Tham telling the visitor to the city that his appearance and manner were a standing invitation to pickpockets.

"I've heard tell about these New York slickers, but they won't get me, you betcha," replied the customer.

"I'll bet thix thenth," said Thubway Tham, "that you've got your coin in a wallet in your hip pocket."

"How'd you know that?" demanded the other suspiciously.

"A man like you alwayth carrieth coin in a wallet in a hip pocket," Tham told him. "It ith a thilly thing to do."

"Where's the best place to carry it?"

"In your inthide vetht pocket," Tham replied. "And don't pull it out where everybody can see it. And don't get drunk."

"Free with your advice, young man, ain't you?" the customer asked. "When I get so I can't attend to my own affairs, I'll retire to an old folks' home."

"That tho?"

"I reckon I've carried my wallet in a hip pocket a good many years, and nobody ever stole it yet."

"All right," said Tham. "Far be it from me to thuggetht anything more."

The customer was mollified. He announced that he would shake dice with Tham for the cigars. Tham agreed, and they shook. The customer from out of town lost a couple of times, and then grew excited. The gambling fever entered the blood of Thubway Tham, too.

They continued to shake dice, and the customer from out of town began winning. He won continually and consistently. Thubway Tham didn't like that — he was getting the house in a bad hole. Almost before he realized it, the customer from out of town had won ten dollars.

He was going to quit, the customer announced. If it was all the same with Tham, he'd take five dollars cash. Tham agreed, since it was a *sub rosa* rule in the store to give customers half their winnings in cash if they so desired.

Tham's boss came back, and the customer hurried away.

"The old coot trimmed me for five," Tham explained, in a manner apologetic.

"Must have shaken dice like a fiend," the boss commented.

"I thought I could rattle 'em, but I couldn't touch him," Tham admitted.

The boss began laughing. "I should think not," he said. "Look here. He went away in a hurry, and he took our dice and left his own."

"Hith own?" Thubway Tham gasped.

"Loaded, you simp! Look here! Try 'em!"

Thubway Tham's face paled.

"Thimp ith right!" he said.

He felt in his vest pocket, took out a five-dollar bill, and put it in the cash register. Then he reached for his hat.

"It's not quitting time yet, young fellow," his boss remarked.

"It ith for me. I have been workin' here for one day, and it hath coth me' forty dollarth. A crook ith an honetht man compared to anybody elthe. I am a thimp! I am an eathy mark! I ought to go and thoak my head! A baby could trim me eathy! Thith ith no place for an honetht crook!"

"Now, see here —"

"I thaid I wath done, and I am! It cotht too much to work in thith plathe. I'm a thimp! I quit!"

Without waiting to argue the matter, Thubway Tham hurried down the street, came to Union Square, and darted toward the entrance to the subway.

A short distance behind, Detective Craddock followed.

II.

A TRAIN roared into the station, and Thubway Tham got aboard. One glance was enough to tell him that there would be no chance for profit during the present trip. There were less than a dozen persons in the car, and none of them appeared to be very prosperous.

Craddock boarded the train also, and Thubway Tham knew it, but gave no sign. He left the train at the Grand Central Station, and Craddock did the same.

"Back to your old tricks, are you?" the detective asked.

"Ain't a man got a right to go to a theater after hith day'th work ith done?" Tham demanded.

"He certainly has, Tham."

"Why don't you thtop petherin' me? Why don't you pether thome-body elthe? I'm an honetht man."

"I hope so, Tham, but I have my doubts. The leopard cannot change his spots, old boy. Going to take a walk?"

"If I am, I don't want you along," Tham told him.

He walked briskly up the street, and on a certain corner came to a stop. He bent forward and looked at a group of men near the curb. And he began chuckling.

He saw the stranger within the city's gates who had beaten him with loaded dice. And he saw the evil-looking youth who had slipped him the counterfeit bill. Thubway Tham knew at a glance that the evil-appearing youth was a crook, that he had spotted the visitor to the city and was hoping to relieve him of his wealth.

Tham leaned back against the corner of the building and watched. Detective Craddock observed Tham's manner and heard his chuckle, and began watching himself. He knew instantly, as did Tham, what the evil-looking youth was going to do. Craddock forgot Tham entirely and gave his attention to the others. Possibly Tham was telling the truth about going straight. And here before Craddock was the situation for a crime.

By watching closely, perhaps Craddock could catch the evil-appearing youth red-handed, so to speak, and earn credit. Craddock had not made many arrests lately, and his captain had made some sarcastic remarks about it.

Craddock stepped back into the shadows and watched closely. So did Tham. After a time the evil-looking youth scientifically removed the wallet from the other's hip pocket. The next instant Detective Craddock had him by the arm.

"I'll just take charge of that wallet, and you too!" Craddock said. "This will cost you a couple of years up the river, my pretty bird!"

The stranger within the city's gates roared his anger. He protested when Craddock put the wallet into his own pocket. He made such a fuss about it that Craddock informed him they would all go to the station and arrange matters there. Since the victim was one of them, they'd go in the subway instead of calling the wagon.

Thubway Tham exulted. One of his enemies had lost a wallet temporarily, and another was in the toils of the law for theft. And there was a chance —

Thubway Tham remembered the forty dollars his day of honest toil had cost him. He wanted that forty, and he needed it. As Detective Craddock started for the nearest subway entrance with his prisoner and the victim, Thubway Tham followed, shadowing the trio as well as ever detective shadowed a suspect.

They got into a crowded car, and Tham kept Craddock from seeing him. And then he began working his way forward, in such a manner as not to attract undue attention to himself. Finally he was two feet behind Detective Craddock in the midst of the crowd.

The proper station was reached, the doors were opened. Detective Craddock started to leave the car with his two men. Thubway Tham stepped up close behind him for an instant — and in that instant his hand dived into Craddock's pocket and took out the countryman's wallet. Chuckling, Tham crept back into the crowd — and the train glided on.

Craddock would find himself in trouble when the station was reached, Tham knew. His evidence against the evil-looking youth would be gone, and by the same token the countryman would demand to be reimbursed for his wallet. Craddock's only explanation would be that he had had his own pocket picked. He might even remember that Thubway Tham had been near at hand, and suspect him — but suspicion would get him nothing. Craddock would have to get Tham "with the goods on" in order to conquer.

Tham left the train at the next station, walked rapidly down the street, then turned into an alley. When he thought it was safe, he investigated the wallet.

There were some newspaper clippings in it, some receipts, but no money.

"Thtung again!" Tham told himself. "Thith ith a rotten day!"

He threw the wallet away from him and went through the alley to the next street. He made his way to a certain saloon, sat at a table in the rear, and brooded over his wrongs. It was getting hard for a prominent pickpocket to make a living, he decided. And it didn't pay to be honest when it cost a man forty dollars a day and his wages were but fifteen a week.

Tham moped for an hour and then went out upon the streets again. He stood on a corner and contemplated a crowd, wondering whether to risk fortune by picking a pocket there. It was against his principles to work anywhere but in the subway, but he told himself that this was all a part of his insane moment.

Somebody slapped him on the shoulder.

"Hey, young fellow!" said a voice in his ear. "Ain't you the cigar clerk?"

Thubway Tham whirled around to face the countryman.

"Hello!" he growled.

"I want to buy you a good cigar. What you told me was right. But I knew it all along. They don't fool me, you betcha. I had a wallet in my hip pocket, all right, but there waren't nothin' except newspaper clippings in it. And a feller picked my pocket and a detective arrested him. And when we got to the police station, the detective had lost the wallet."

"Huh!" Tham said, this not being news to him.

"I reckon these New York slickers don't get gay with me! You know what I did, young feller? I raised Cain, I did! I said as how there was a hundred dollars in that wallet, and I demanded that the detective pay me back. He argued some about it and then took me to another room, and we argued some more. Finally he give me fifty, and I called it square. I reckon these New York slickers don't get the best of me!"

"You made him pay you fifty?" Tham queried with a gasp.

"I certainly did — and there wasn't nothin' in that there wallet except clippings. He had to let that pickpocket go, too. I'm wise, you betcha. I been carryin' my real money in my vest pocket all the time, bills folded up."

"You're withe, all right," Tham said. "Carryin' it in your vetht pocket all the time, eh?"

"Sure! And I've got that detective's fifty there with it. If this keeps up, young feller, I'll have all my expenses paid and go home with a profit."

Thubway Tham chuckled until the tears started from his eyes. He'd have to tell Craddock about this some time, he promised himself. It certainly would be rubbing it in so far as Craddock was concerned.

"You don't owe me any cigar," he told the countryman. "That ith a good joke, and I'll buy you a drink. Come along."

He led the way to the nearest resort that had plenty of bright lights. He ordered drinks and paid for them, and whispered to the countryman about the joke, and they had more drinks and laughed aloud at Detective Craddock.

"I know a better place than this," Tham said and led the way.

But it seemed impossible to get a finger into that vest pocket where the countryman kept the currency. It was not that the visitor to the city was on guard, particularly, but luck was against Tham.

They went along a dark side street, but Tham had no chance to get the money. He tried to get his man intoxicated in another resort, but found that he could not.

So they drifted about the city for two hours, and finally Thubway Tham began to have hopes.

The countryman began exhibiting the first signs of intoxication. Tham decided that he'd make the attempt soon now. And then the visitor to the city took the wind out of his sails.

"You look like an honest young feller," he said. "And you know all about this town. I can't enjoy myself while I'm worryin' about my money. You take it — here — and keep it for me. Give me a bill whenever I ask for it."

"Nothin' doin'," said Thubway Tham.

"You take it!" the other commanded, pressing it upon him.

"All right," Tham said, in a voice of resignation.

"You see, I ain't afraid of you, young feller. I know where you work. If you run off with that money, I'd just go to that cigar store tomorrow and get it, you betcha!"

"Yeth?" Tham risked.

Thubway Tham was astounded. Here was a man trusting him with money — the man he had hoped to rob. He glanced at the bills and saw that they totaled more than a hundred dollars, and fifty dollars of it, he supposed, was Craddock's.

The situation appealed to Thubway Tham. He knew that he could evade the countryman in some resort that had doors opening onto two streets, but he decided to be honest for the time being.

"Thith ith thertainly my inthane moment," he told himself. "I mutht be gettin' old or thomethin' like that!"

He followed the countryman for two hours more. They changed some of the bills, but when midnight came, and the visitor decided that he would return to his hotel and go to bed, there remained something like seventy-five dollars. Thubway Tham handed it back, made the other count it and acknowledge the amount correct, and then parted from his man with a feeling that he had done a worthy action.

He drifted into one of the saloons they had patronized earlier in the evening, and the proprietor hailed him.

"You can't play any game like this on me, Tham," he said.

"What ith the matter with you?"

"You were in here with a friend — fellow who looked like a hick. You bought the drinks and changed a ten. And the ten is a bad one — that's what's the matter with me."

Tham glanced into the man's face and knew that he spoke the truth.

"That wath not my money," he said. "I've been thtung again! And by a hick! Here's a good ten for it. Great Thcott!"

Tham had a horrible idea. Were all the bills he had passed counterfeit? Had the visitor to the city played him for an easy mark, got him to pass the money so that, if an arrest came, Tham would be the one arrested?

And Thubway Tham was known well in all the places where he had changed bills. The proprietors would be quick to complain about it. Crooks themselves, for the most part, they would not have another crook play them.

With a heavy heart Thubway Tham began making the rounds. It was as he had expected — several men called him to account. Thubway Tham gave good bills and collected the bad ones, and explained how he had been worked. That was the worst of it — he had to explain to square himself; he had to admit that he had been played for an easy mark!

He handed over all the good money he possessed. In the last place, he could not replace a bad five, but he explained and promised to do so the following day. And then, with rage in his heart, he walked toward Union Square.

Thubway Tham was deadly angry now. He plunged into the subway, got into a crowded car, "lifted a leather," and got out at Twenty-eighth street. He walked up to the next station, entered the subway again, lifted another leather, and got out at Times Square. He took out bills and dropped the wallets. Thubway Tham was collecting for the misfortunes of the day.

It was two o'clock in the morning when he entered the dingy room far downtown, the room that was his home. He investigated and found that the proceeds of the night's work amounted to more than two hundred dollars.

"Played for a thucker by a hick!" he exclaimed. "It doth not pay to try to be honetht! Inthane moment ith ethactly right! But it ith a good joke on Craddock!"

THUBWAY THAM'S
THANKSGIVING DINNER

THUBWAY THAM stood across the street from Union Square, his mouth drooping at the corners, his general appearance that of a man who did not have a friend in the world and but few relatives.

You are acquainted with Thubway Tham, of course, the clever little pickpocket who lisped and who worked at his nefarious pursuit only in the subway during rush hours, two facts that caused his nickname to come into being. That name now was one to conjure with in the city's underworld.

On this, the day before the annual Thanksgiving feast, Thubway Tham leaned against the wall of a building and almost snarled as he looked at the jostling throngs. He scarcely knew whether to weep or curse. He felt that he was experiencing mingled friendlessness, loneliness, and the old-fashioned blues. Thubway Tham was at the point where a man begins to pity himself.

"Well, well, if it isn't my old friend, Tham!" said a voice at his elbow. There was a certain amount of sarcasm in the voice, and Thubway Tham grunted his displeasure as he whirled around to face Detective Craddock.

Craddock knew Thubway Tham for what he was. He had sworn to "get" Thubway Tham and to see that he spent a long term in the big, cold prison up the river. But at every crisis Thubway Tham appeared to be favored of the gods to such an extent that he always escaped. Detective Craddock, to get Thubway Tham, had to "catch him with the goods," and he knew it.

"Thith ith enough," Thubway Tham said now. "Thith ith the latht thtraw! Now I am goin' to butht thomething wide open! Jutht ath I wath moanin' to mythelf about not havin' any friendth for Thankthgivin', you come along with your ugly fathe and make me feel worthe! Thith ith the lath thtraw!"

"Why, Tham, you're not homesick, or anything like that, are you?"

"I ain't even got a home to be homethick about, you poor thimp!"

"Remorseful because of your mode of life, Tham, old boy?"

"You make me thick," Tham complained. "I ain't got any mode of life, whatever that ith! I ain't nobody and I ain't got nuthin! I'm jutht a thilly ath!"

"Aren't you a bit hard on yourself, Tham?"

"And you —" Tham sputtered in his wrath. "You — all you do ith pethter me to death. You follow me around like a dog thmellin' a thteak. I don't thee why they have to have Thankthgivin' anyway. Thilly old idea!"

"Why, Tham, on that day we give thanks because we have had a year of plenty."

"I've had plenty of you the patht year, all right," Tham told him. "It ain't right for a man to be pethtered all the time by the thame fly cop!"

"You know why, Tham. You're going to make a little slip one of these days, and then you are going up the river. It can't last, Tham, old rooster!"

"If I made thith thlip right under your nothe, you wouldn't thee it," Tham told him. He started to move away.

"Going to take a little ride in the subway, Tham?" Craddock asked. "Because, if you are, I'm going right along. It appears that about every time you take a ride in the subway, some gentleman of means reports that his pocketbook is unaccountably missing."

"I thuppothe I am to blame for every purthe in town that ith thlit," Tham said.

"Perhaps not every purse, Tham, old boy, but for quite a quantity of them."

"Thay! I am on the thquare today, and I don't want to be pethtered. I ain't feelin' well," Thubway Tham explained. "Maybe it ith my thtom-ach."

"Don't let it be your nerves, Tham. If those fingers of yours begin to itch and tingle, they might get you into trouble. However, you may be a clever dip, but you are not a liar. If you tell me on your word of honor that you are in a blown funk today and do not intend to work, I'll go about my business and leave you alone."

"You got my word," Tham said.

Detective Craddock made an elaborate bow.

"In that case, Tham, go your way in peace," he said. "But may Heaven help you if I find later that I have been double crossed!"

"Did I ever double crothe anybody?" Tham angrily demanded. "Don't I alwayth play thquare? Don't you forget that I'm an honetht crook! Double crothe! You make me thick! Thilly ath!"

Thubway Tham turned his back upon Detective Craddock's laughing face and walked away. He felt the grip of a great loneliness upon him again. It was true that he did not have a relative in all the world, and such friends as he possessed were friends of short standing — acquaintances, rather — and were not to be trusted too far. The only time Thubway Tham had been "sent away" was through a stool pigeon he had taken to his bosom, believing him to be an honest man.

He walked on around Union Square, and finally came to a stop before a large restaurant and café. It was time to eat, but Thubway Tham was no slave to habit; he ate when hunger called for food and not at stated hours.

He glanced through a big window and watched the diners. On the morrow, he knew, several thousand would eat their Thanksgiving dinners in that restaurant, and almost all of them would be eating it with friends. Tham could not remember when he had eaten one except alone, and again his heart grew sad.

He appeared to come to a sudden decision, for he hurried through the door and declared that he wished to speak to the manager. The cashier sent for his superior.

"I want to order a Thankthgiving dinner," Thubway Tham told him.

"Yes, sir — glad to serve you, sir," the manager said, he glanced at Thubway Tham's clothes, which were not of the costliest, but the manager knew better than to judge solely by a man's clothes.

"A regular dinner for ten," Thubway Tham went on. "I want the whole thtuff, with all the trimmin'. And I want the oythterth jutht right and the thelery crithp!"

"I shall make it a point to see that you are well served, sir."

"I want that dinner ready at one o'clock," Tham went on. "Ten of uth — at a thpecial table."

"Yes, sir. We can do it for a dollar and a half a plate, sir."

"Thay! I want a dinner," Thubway Tham said. "I want thomething extra thpethial! And, now that I come to think of it, we'll make that dinner for twenty — five dollarth a plate."

"Dinner for twenty — one hundred dollars — yes, sir. And — er — it is usual in such cases for a little deposit —"

"Of courthe," said Tham. He took two ten-dollar bills from his pocket and extended them. "I'll pay you the retht tomorrow when I come to dinner."

"Thank you, sir — that will be satisfactory. And the name?"

"Joneth," said Thubway Tham.

II.

THUBWAY THAM'S breast was swollen like that of a pouter pigeon as he went out upon the street. He had talked and acted like a man of substance. He actually had ordered a dinner for nineteen friends and himself, a dinner that was to cost one hundred dollars, and he had paid twenty dollars down in advance to make sure of the service.

"All I got to do now ith to get nineteen friendth and eighty dollarth," he told himself.

He didn't know where to turn to get his guests and, as for the eighty dollars, he had given his word to Detective Craddock that he would not enter his beloved subway this day with the object of relieving some gentleman of his valuables.

Thubway Tham spent another hour wandering around the streets and considering this problem. And then he thought of newsboys.

It often had appeared to Thubway Tham that Thanksgiving Day was a national institution for newsboys. When the holiday approached, almost everybody planned a dinner for newsies he knew, and grinning ladies and gentlemen stood about the tables and watched them gorge themselves.

Tham knew that some of the newspapers furnished these dinners, and he guessed that the newsies grew tired of them at times. He decided to invite nineteen of them to a special dinner, where they would be treated as honored guests instead of objects of wonder.

Thubway Tham found that the first newsie he approached looked upon him with suspicion. But finally he made himself clear, and the newsie was delighted. He spoke for himself and four friends, and he directed Thubway Tham to a boy on a certain other corner who could supply more guests. Thubway Tham spent another two hours delivering personal invitations to the special dinner to be given by "Mr. Joneth" at a certain restaurant at a certain hour the following day.

That night Tham felt some nervousness as he thought of it. Being host at a dinner for twenty was something new in the life of Thubway Tham. And he had less than two dollars in his pocket, and would have to hand the restaurant manager eighty before his guests could be served. In the event of failure, Thubway Tham could merely remain away from the restaurant and ignore his guests, of course, but Thubway Tham was a gentleman of honor in some things. He had invited guests to a dinner, and he would supply the dinner and funds to pay for it.

IT WAS eight o'clock on the morning of Thanksgiving Day when Thubway Tham, dressed as carefully and as elaborately as possibly, entered the subway far downtown, where he lived, and caught a train bound for a district up the island.

His lips curled into a sneer as he looked at the others in the car. There was small chance here for Thubway Tham to get his eighty dollars, the crowd having the appearance of not possessing one-tenth that sum.

Thubway Tham rode to Times Square and emerged upon the street. There seemed to be a sort of unsettled look about the city. Thubway Tham realized that it was because this was a holiday. The same old crowds were not in the same old places at the same hours. The routine of the city was disrupted.

And then a thought of horror came to him. Perhaps because of this condition, there would be no jostling crowds no rush hours in the subway. There would be large theater crowds at the matinee hour, of course, but that would be too late for his purpose. Tham had ordered dinner for one o'clock.

He plunged into the subway again and rode down one station to

Grand Central. There were less than half a dozen persons in the car in which he rode, and when the station was reached he found that there was no jostling crowd there. And there he felt a touch on his arm, and whirled around to find Detective Craddock at his elbow.

"Enjoying Thanksgiving, Tham?" Craddock asked. "It's a great old holiday! But don't you think you are a bit far uptown?"

"I've got a perfect, right —" Tham began.

"I know you have, Tham. As I remarked on a previous occasion, your right certainly is perfect — meaning the right hand and the manner in which it can invade a man's pocket, of course. And your left isn't so bad, either."

"Thay! Are you goin' to pethter me again today?" Thubway demanded. "It ith bad enough to have no friendth or relativeth on thuth a day, without bein' pethtered too. It ith about all a man can thtand!"

"Ah! Want to make another little promise pact — word of honor until the holiday is over, or something like that?"

"I do not make any dealth with the devil," Thubway Tham told him. "You talk like a thilly ath!"

"Ah! That means of course, that you are out for the stuff today, since you refuse to give me your word you'll do nothing wrong. Well, I suppose I'll have to toddle along right behind you and protect the wallets of the public."

"Thay! I am gettin' thick of thith! You thtay away from me onthe in a while!"

"Can't afford to do it, Tham. I've got to be handy when you make that slip, you know."

"You and your thlipth!"

"Now, don't get angry, Tham. A man never is fully efficient when he is angry, and when a man is not efficient, slips occur. You want to watch out for that slip, Tham, for if you give the judge a chance he's going to hang quite a number of years on your record."

"If I let you catch me, I ought to get a million yearth," Tham told him.

"Want to make that promise of yours good for today, then?"

"No, thir! I don't promithe nuthin'!"

"On the warpath then, are you?"

"Yeth, thir — I am!"

III.

A TRAIN was just roaring into the station. Tham entered a car, Detective Craddock following, went through it rapidly, and sprang through the doorway and out just as the door started to close. But Craddock got out, too.

"A little slow that time, Tham," he said. "You worked that trick on me once, you know."

Thubway Tham made no reply. He was thoroughly angry now. It was almost ten o'clock in the morning, and Tham had to have eighty dollars before one o'clock to keep faith with the guests he had invited. He was commencing to feel desperate. Three hours was a short time in which to accomplish his purpose, especially when the subway crowds were not what they should have been and Detective Craddock was at his heels.

He ascended to the street and for half an hour dodged here and there, but failed to evade Craddock. It appeared that the detective was determined this day — he did not intend to lose sight of Thubway Tham. They did not speak, but now and then they glared at each other.

Tham went over to Broadway again and sought a crowd into which he could plunge and shake off Craddock, but Broadway did not seem to be dealing in crowds today. So Tham gave a sigh of resignation, went into the subway again, and traveled to Union Square.

Craddock was two paces behind him when he went up to the street, and stood looking at the battleship replica and the blue jackets around it. Tham saw one of the newsboys he had invited to dinner, and the newsie stopped work long enough to wave a hand at him and grin.

Why, they were anticipating that dinner, Tham told himself. He had made friends merely by inviting them. They'd speak to him after this whenever he passed them on the street. He'd have friends!

But, unless he got the eighty dollars, what then? They'd point him out with scorn as the man who invited nineteen newsboys to a Thanksgiving dinner and then did not show up to furnish the food.

Thubway Tham felt a lump come into his throat, and it startled him, for he had not believed himself capable of emotion. Why, he simply had to get that eighty dollars, he told himself! He couldn't fool those expectant newsboys! If that confounded Craddock —

He turned around to find Craddock grinning at him. It was almost as if the detective had read his thoughts. Thubway Tham never resorted to violence in his work, but he felt now that he would like to have Detective Craddock walking through a dark alley and be waiting there himself with a club in his hands.

He started walking around the square. Craddock followed, of course. Tham glanced at his watch, and saw that it was almost eleven o'clock. He had only two hours.

Once more he turned toward the subway entrance, this time to find some sort of a crowd there. Thubway Tham plunged into it gracefully, like a swimmer plunging into the ocean's ample waters. He darted here and there on the platform below. A train dashed in, and Thubway Tham got into one of the cars without Craddock noticing him. The train started. Thubway Tham caught a glimpse of Craddock on the platform outside, and Craddock saw him. But Thubway Tham was on an express train, and Craddock would have to wait for the next — nor did he know at which station Thubway Tham would get off.

Tham scarcely knew that himself. He decided, finally, to change and go as far uptown as Columbus Circle. That was territory that meant trouble if Craddock saw him there, for Thubway Tham had been warned to remain away from that district. The warning had followed some particularly bold thefts around the Columbus Circle station.

Tham was gratified to find this train was more crowded than the others had been. He left his seat and stood not far from one of the doors. He saw an elderly gentleman of prosperous appearance in whose face was reflected the spirit of the holiday. Tham felt sure the elderly gentleman could afford to lose a few dollars, and that perhaps he was the sort of man who would have fed a group of newsboys himself, had he happened to think of it.

The train stopped, and the crowd surged from the cars. Thubway Tham brushed against the elderly gentleman for a moment, and an instant later he had a fat wallet in his own pocket.

Thubway Tham's heart exulted as he reached the street. He could return to Union Square and keep faith with his newsies now. He could eat with them, and make sure that they enjoyed it, and he would make friends.

He made his way quickly to a convenient saloon, sat down at a table, and ordered a drink. Waiting until he was sure that nobody was observing him, he took the wallet from his pocket. He wanted to remove the money and get rid of the damning purse; it wouldn't do to have Craddock or some other detective find that on his person. As for the money itself, bills are hard to identify.

He opened the wallet and searched it quickly. And once more hope fled his breast.

The wallet contained no money at all. In it were newspaper and magazine clippings furnished by a clipping bureau, all having to do with some art collection.

Thubway Tham was almost sobbing now. He looked at his watch again and found that it was noon. Within a few minutes his guests would be gathering at the restaurant in Union Square. They would wait patiently for him at first, and then doubt would begin to enter their hearts; finally they would decide that Thubway Tham had worked a cruel hoax on them.

Tham considered his watch. At a certain place far downtown he could get ten dollars on that watch; he knew, because he often had done it before. But ten dollars would do no good in the present emergency.

He tried to think of other resources, and failed to do so. Given several hours, he might have been able to borrow the sum in small amounts from acquaintances in the underworld, but he did not have time for that.

Thubway Tham threw the wallet into a cuspidor and hurried from the place. He went into the subway again, traveled downtown, and got out at Union Square. And there he met Craddock again.

"You've got to stand a frisk, Tham," Craddock told him. "You went uptown, and it's a safe bet that you nicked somebody for his roll."

"Thearch me," said Tham.

"This is no bluff, Tham. I intend to do it. Stand back here!"

Craddock searched and found a dollar bill and some change, and that was all.

"Thee?" Tham asked him. "I just got enough to get my Thankth-givin' dinner."

"Um! How does it come you are so nearly broke, Tham?"

"Expentheth ith thomething awful," Tham explained. "I gueth I will have to get a job thome plathe."

"Well, why not?"

"If I did you'd pethter me jutht the thame," Tham told him. "I thuppothe I am due to be pethtered by you ath long ath I live in thith town."

"Huh! Why not move?"

"And leave the thubway?" Tham asked.

Such a thought was horrifying. Since the day when it had been thrown open for the use of the public, Thubway Tham had worshiped the big line. Life away from the subway was something too awful for Tham to contemplate.

He wished Craddock would leave him. It was almost one o'clock, and Tham knew that the newsboys were gathering for the feast he had promised them. He wished now he had had only ten guests at a dollar and a half a plate, but it was too late for that now.

"Tham, if you're really broke, I can slip you a five," Craddock told him. "I expect to send you up the river some day, but I can't get any glory out of tracking down a hungry man. A hungry man, you know, will make mistakes a man who has had his dinner will not make. This is a square fight between us, Tham."

"You couldn't make it eighty dollarth, could you?" Tham asked.

"Do you think I'm the First National Bank, my boy? Why do you want eighty dollars?"

"Oh, I don't," said Tham quickly. "I wath jutht talkin'. Thankth for your kindneth, but I can get along without the five."

"Well, be mighty careful how you replenish your funds, Tham."

"You jutht keep your eyeth open," Tham advised him. "I can borrow, and I can collect what thome men owe me. And I can get me a job thome plathe when all other hope ith gone."

Thubway Tham turned away — and Detective Craddock turned after him. Tham was near to tears. Why, he'd not dare look a newsie in the face after this, he told himself. They'd hate the sight of him. And he didn't have the nerve to go across to the restaurant and tell them the truth; he knew what sort of a reception that would earn for him.

He passed the subway entrance, where there was quite a throng now, and Craddock moved closer. But, Tham continued on through the crowd instead of going underground.

And then the heart of Thubway Tham almost ceased beating. In front of him a man was getting out of a taxi-cab. He paid the chauffeur from a roll of bills and thrust the remaining bills carelessly into the outside pocket of his overcoat. Thubway Tham, desperate, willing to take a chance despite the nearness of Detective Craddock, darted his hand forward and got the bills, transferred them to his own pocket, and went on through the crowd with Craddock at his heels. He walked briskly toward the restaurant, and once, where there was another crowd, he glanced at the bills to find he had ample for his present needs.

"And I did it right under hith thilly nothe!" Tham exultingly told himself. He turned and faced Craddock boldly. "I am going in thith plathe to get my Thankthgivin' dinner, and I don't want you around," he told the detective. "I ain't got much money and I want to enjoy my meal. And I can't do it if you are near. You give me indigethtion."

"Fair enough, Tham. Go ahead and eat!" Craddock said.

Tham turned into the restaurant.

"Ah, Mr. Jones, we were beginning to get a bit worried about you," the manager said. "Your little guests are here, and looking hungry."

"Here ith the eighty," Tham told him, and counted out the bills, finding that he had some fifteen dollars remaining. And then he hurried to the long table where nineteen grinning newsies shouted a welcome that warmed Thubway Tham's heart.

The manager stepped to the door and nodded to Detective Craddock. "There's the kind of man I like," he said.

"Who's that?" Craddock asked.

"At the head of the long table back there. He's giving a dinner to nineteen newsboys. I was a bit leary of him for a time, but he's all right. Showed up at the last minute and paid me the eighty dollars he owed for the dinner."

"Just now?" Craddock asked.

"Sure!"

"And when I searched him less than ten minutes ago he didn't have two dollars in his clothes. And he spoke to me about borrowing eighty. I wonder where he got it?"

One of the newsies hurried out and handed Craddock a cigar.

"Mr. Jones sent it to you, sir," the boy explained, "He's giving us a dinner, and he's some prince. And he said that, if you were hungry, to come in and he'd have another plate set."

Detective Craddock snorted.

"You tell your friend Mr. Jones," he said, "that I'll get him yet!"

"Yes, sir."

"And I hope all of you enjoy your dinner. I don't care to eat just now. You see, I'm afraid I couldn't relish the grub just at the present time."

THUBWAY THAM'S
UNDERSTUDY

THUBWAY THAM, the clever little pickpocket who worked only in the subway, who lisped when he talked and called himself Thubway Tham and wanted other men to do the same — Thubway Tham, on this pleasant morning, paced the floor of the dingy room he called home, and frowned, and now and then smote with a fist the opposite palm, and yet chuckled at intervals.

If you know anything at all about Thubway Tham, you know that a certain city detective, Craddock by name, had sworn to get Thubway Tham "with the goods" and see that he served a long term in the big prison up the river. Now, in order to exist properly, a pickpocket must work the same as men in other walks of life. Make it impossible for him to work, and it is going to be difficult for him to pay room rent and purchase food and clothing. And that is exactly what had happened to Thubway Tham.

For the past two weeks, Craddock had trailed him so closely and so well that Thubway Tham had been unable to "lift a leather." His meager funds were exhausted, and Thubway Tham either had to resort to some sort of strategy or go to work in some honest line of endeavor, which latter by no means appealed to him.

And so Thubway Tham had decided to resort to strategy. He had the acquaintance of a youth of the underworld known as Shifty Peter. This budding criminal was like a boy just out of college — he was undecided what to make his life work. At times he thought he would become a burglar, and then he heard that burglars were having a particularly bad time of it. Then he would almost decide to become a second-story man, and have somebody tell him that there was no class to that part of the profession.

While trying to decide what course to pursue to fame and fortune, Shifty Peter played at being a sneak thief and managed in some way to live. He admired Thubway Tham, as did others of the underworld — and finally decided that he would become a pickpocket and work his way to the top of the trade.

Thubway Tham formed what he considered an excellent plot. Shifty Peter would be his understudy. It was a known thing in the underworld that the subway was the special ground of Thubway Tham, and other criminals were to keep away, especially other pickpockets. The police, if a crime was reported from the subway, always credited it to Thubway Tham therefore, and orders had gone forth to get him.

Now Thubway Tham intended to let Detective Craddock hang about his heels so well that he could not commit a crime, but Shifty Peter would commit crimes, and in the subway. Therefore Craddock would know that all wallets stolen there did not find their way to the pockets of Thubway Tham. The impression would go forth that Tham was not entirely to be blamed for all subway thefts. Moreover, the attention of Craddock would be distracted, and then Thubway Tham could work himself.

In return for having been taught certain tricks of the trade, and for the protection Thubway Tham could give him, Shifty Peter was to hand to Tham one-half of all the proceeds. This arrangement would give Tham expense money while Craddock was being properly mystified. Shifty Peter had agreed to this without reservation.

On this morning the test was to be made. Thubway Tham ceased pacing the floor when he heard a knock at the door. He listened, and heard a peculiar hiss that only Shifty Peter could give. Thubway Tham opened the door and let Peter shuffle into the room.

"Everything ready?" Peter asked.

"Yeth," Tham replied. "We will try it thith noon at the ruth hour. Ath my underthtudy, I expect you to not dithgrathe me. You mutht not be nervouth. Keep cool, Thifty, and never play the thimp! Uthe judgment when you pick your man! Remember all I have told you, and you'll get along all right!"

"Don't you go to worrying about me, Tham, old boy!" Shifty Peter told him.

"You get too confident and you'll probably go to jail!" Tham said.

"Pickin' a pocket ith no eathy thtunt! The betht of uth make mithtaketh, and you're only an amateur!"

"Oh, I'll be careful, Tham."

"Then we'll thtart. I thuppothe that thilly ath of a Craddock will be waitin' on the corner to pick me up. He'th even got a man helpin' him now. It ith gettin' to be tho an honetht crook can't make a livin'."

"You said a mouthful there, old-timer!"

Thubway Tham glared at him. "Don't get freth!" he warned. "Thith ith no eathy buthineth! You remember everything I told you, and pay attention to your work! And you watch out for Craddock, too! Now, we'll thtart!"

They left the room, and Shifty Peter went down the rear stairs to the alley, through the alley to the street, and loitered near the corner. Detective Craddock was there, but he gave Peter no attention at all. Craddock was after Thubway Tham.

Tham went down the front stairs and turned the corner. Craddock met him face to face and grinned.

"Good morning, Tham!" he said.

"It ith not a good morning when I thee your ugly fathe!" Tham replied.

"In a bad humor, eh? Maybe you didn't sleep good last night; or are you having domestic troubles?"

"I thlept all right, and I ain't got anybody to have domethtic troubleth with!" Tham told him. "But I get chronic dythpepthia whenever I thee you! You are ruinin' my thtomach, man!"

"Well, I'm sorry, Tham. But you're not using your stomach much these days anyway, are you?"

"No?"

"No!" said Craddock. "Your day's work is about done, Tham. We are keeping our eyes on you. You don't nick any more men for their rolls in the subway, old boy!"

"Thay — !"

"Now please do not start singing that old song about being an innocent and misunderstood man, Tham! We're wise to you!"

"Yeth?"

"Yes!"

"Are you goin' to pethter me again today?" Thubway Tham demanded. "Mutht I put up with it?"

"I like your companionship so much, Tham," Craddock said, "that I insist upon going wherever you go, until you start on your trip up the river."

"Yeth?"

"Yes! You had my goat for a while, Tham, but I've got it back now — and maybe yours along with it."

"Well, my goodneth! Lithten to the man!" Thubway Tham said to the world at large. "It taketh a mighty good man to get my goat, a better man than any on the polithe forthe!"

"So?" said Craddock.

"Tho! I'll have to thlow down a lot before anybody getth my goat! No thimp of a cop can do it! Thome of theth dayth, Craddock, you are goin' to make me mad. And then there ith goin' to be one awful fight, and a vacanthy on the forthe — a big hole where onthe you were!"

"Oh, I'm not alarmed, Tham!" Craddock said, looking down at him and laughing. "By the way, were you thinking of riding on the subway this morning?"

"I thertainly am!"

"Better take the elevated or surface cars, Tham — or walk. It makes us nervous to have you in the subway."

"That ith nothin' in my young life!"

"If you insist upon taking the subway, Tham, I'll have to trot right along with you," said Craddock.

"If you want to thpend your money on thubway ticketth, it ith none of my buthineth," Tham told him.

"Oh, it is expense money, Tham, old boy — city money."

"No wonder the tackthpayerth ith alwayth howlin'!" Tham told him. He turned his back and made for the nearest subway entrance. Detective Craddock trotted along at his heels.

Shifty Peter trailed them both, rapidly approaching them.

II.

THUBWAY THAM entered the subway and took a train uptown. Detective Craddock and Shifty Peter got into the same car, Craddock within half a dozen feet of Tham, and Shifty Peter at the other end. Before they had passed three stations, the car was jammed.

Thubway Tham was standing facing Craddock, with whom he maintained a conversation, and from this position he could watch Shifty Peter easily. Being an experienced pickpocket, and having trained this understudy himself, Thubway Tham instantly spotted the man Peter had selected as a victim. Thubway Tham was well pleased with the novice: It was such a man as he himself might have selected, a man whose appearance indicated prosperity and carelessness.

"You make me thick!" he was telling Craddock. "Who ever gave you a lithenthe to be a detective? You follow me around like a hound thmellin' a thteak, and while you're doin' that thome dip probably ith gettin' away with thomething thome plathe elthe."

"Don't let that worry you, Tham, old boy. I'm not the only man on the force."

"You act it at timeth," Thubway Tham told him. "Jutht becauthe onthe I wath caught, you blame everything on me. Every time a purthe ith thnatched in the thubway, of courthe it ith Tham who did it!"

"That's what we think."

"Yeth! That ith what you think! It ith eathier to blame it on me than to look for the real crook! You make me thick!"

"You'll be still sicker on the day you make a little slip and I nab you and start you up the river."

"Tho? Jutht you remember thith, Craddock — I ain't to blame for everything that happenth!"

Even as he spoke, from the corner of one eye he saw Shifty Peter do his work. Thubway Tham found himself admiring the technic of his young understudy. Shifty Peter had extracted a wallet in the most approved manner, and had transferred it to his own pocket. He had done it just as the train came into a station, and had already moved a dozen feet away from his victim and was preparing to leave the train.

Thubway Tham decided to leave it also. He followed Peter to the street, Craddock walking a pace behind him. They were at Times Square, in the midst of a throng.

"Tham," Craddock said, "I suppose you are going to attempt to dodge me in the crowd, so you can get back in the subway and lift a leather or two. Listen to me, boy — I'm sticking closer to you today than a silk undershirt. I have had words with the inspector, boy, and he made the remark that I had to curb your activities or look for a new job of some sort. You grasp me, Tham?"

"I grathp you, all right," Thubway Tham told him. "And you can jutht thtick ath clothe ath you pleathe! Nothing would pleathe me more!"

"Tham, this is sarcasm,"Craddock accused.

But it was not sarcasm. For once, Thubway Tham meant it. He wanted Craddock to stick close to him. He wanted Craddock to know that he had not "turned a trick." Then he wanted Craddock to discover, when he returned to police headquarters, that there had been several robberies in the subway.

In a very deft manner, Thubway Tham conveyed a signal to Shifty Peter, who was halfway up the block. Peter immediately started walking down Seventh Avenue. Tham started that way himself, and Craddock, whistling softly, paced beside him.

"Thtick jutht ath clothe ath pothible!" Tham told the detective. "Ath clothe ath a thilk underthirt!"

Shifty Peter set a good pace, and Tham kept within half a block of him. Block after block they went, until they came to the vicinity of the Pennsylvania Station. Tham sent another signal to Shifty Peter, who turned into the station and went down to the subway platform.

Again the three of them got into the same car, Tham and Craddock at one end, and Peter at the other. Again the car was crowded. Tham maintained a conversation and watched his understudy. Once more, he was agreeably surprised to see with what skill Shifty Peter worked. The youth made an excellent protégé, Tham thought. He would be a credit to the profession if he kept a level head.

Just before Fourteenth Street was reached, Shifty Peter did something of which Tham did not approve. He lifted another leather. It made

Tham angry. He had explained to Peter that a man should lift a leather just as a station was reached and the car was in a turmoil, then leave the train immediately and get as far as possible from the victim with great speed. Lift a leather, take out the money, and get rid of the purse. Then it was time enough to think of repeating the performance.

Shifty Peter, however, had continued on the train after getting the first wallet, riding a dozen feet from his victim, in danger of being searched and caught with the goods if the victim discovered his loss and raised a cry. Moreover, he had obtained a second purse before disposing of the first.

Thubway Tham promised himself that he would read Peter a lecture as soon as he got him alone. He saw that Peter intended leaving the train at Fourteenth Street and prepared to do likewise. Up to the street they went, Craddock at Tham's elbow.

"What is the idea of this globe-trotting tour?" Craddock wanted to know.

"I am a good thitithen," Tham explained. "I thupport every in-duthtry I can. And how can you eckthpect the thubway to make a livin' if people don't ride in it?"

"Very charitable on your part, Tham. What are we going to do now?"

"I am going home to retht."

"Now, Tham, you know very well that I'll go right along and stand on the corner and watch for you to come out again."

"Thtand on the corner all you pleathe!" Tham told him.

He gave Shifty Peter another signal and started down the street. Peter quickened his pace and hurried on ahead. Thubway Tham walked leisurely and refused to hold further conversation with the grinning Craddock. Tham appeared to be angry. He wanted Craddock to believe that he had given up in disgust all idea of lifting a leather this day because of Craddock's presence.

He came to the lodging house and went up the stairs. He walked through the office and then went to the end of the front hall and glanced down at the street. Craddock was standing on the corner, from where he could watch both entrances to the place. Tham hurried up to his room.

Shifty Peter was there. On the bed were three wallets, and Peter was extracting their contents.

"You ath!" Tham broke out, whirling around, slamming the door and locking it. "Tryin' to get in jail? Why did you bring them thingth here? Didn't I tell you to get rid of the leatherth ath thoon ath pothible? And here you thit, like an ath, with the door unlocked, gloatin' over them. Thuppothe Craddock had come up with me to take a look around! Oh, you thilly ath!"

"Gosh, I never thought of that!" Peter said.

"You want to think, boy, or it thoon will be curtainth for you!" Tham replied. "Thpill out them billth and get out of here with the walletth. Get rid of them, and don't do it around the houthe, either. Then come back and we'll thplit!"

"Why not split now?" Peter asked.

"Do ath I thay!" Tham commanded. "Do you think I won't thplit even?"

Thubway Tham suddenly became menacing. He did not like the idea of a fellow crook imagining him crooked. Shifty Peter cringed against the wall.

"I'll — I'll go!" he wailed.

He sprang to the bed, emptied the wallets, handed the mass of bills to Tham, stuffed the empty wallets into his pocket, and bolted through the door.

Tham locked the door again and counted the swag.

"Two hundred and ten dollarth!" he whispered. "The boy ith all right, but he ith liable to cauthe me trouble if he ith not more careful. Runnin' a rithk like that — the thimp!"

III.

UPON THE following morning, Tham looked from the window of his room to see Shifty Peter standing across the street. Peter made a signal which meant that Detective Craddock was at the corner waiting to attach himself to Tham when he emerged, and Tham replied with another signal which meant that he would be out in a few minutes.

He had given Peter a lecture the day before when the youth returned for his share of the receipts. Peter had accepted the rebuke with good grace, especially since he had a hundred and five dollars as the result of Tham's teachings.

"The betht way to pull off a thtunt ith right under the nothe of the polithe!" Tham had said. "I alwayth thaid tho, and now I know it!"

He swaggered from the lodging house and started up the street, ignoring Detective Craddock purposely, but Craddock caught up with him before he reached the end of the block.

"Good morning, Tham!" he said.

"My he02enth!" Tham groaned. "You thpoil every day of my life! Here ith your ugly fathe again before I have had my breakfatht!"

"Business, Tham."

"I thuppothe you want to thearch me or thomething like that?" Tham said. "I thuppothe thomebody in Than Franthithco wath touched latht night for hith roll, and you think I did it!"

"Why, Tham, how sarcastic. Surely you are not sleeping well these days. I just wanted to say, Tham, that somebody is working your district."

"I don't grathp you."

"Tham, I was sticking mighty close to you yesterday, and I know blamed well that you didn't get your hands into anybody's pockets except your own. And yet, Tham, old boy, three gentlemen were relieved of their purses in the subway at about the same time I was with you."

"Well, my he02enth!"

"I guess they are beginning to think you are done, Tham. You're slowing up, they think. Somebody surely is working the district that is supposed to be yours."

"Me, thlow up?" Thubway Tham gasped. "Not for yearth yet! Man, I am jutht gettin' into my thtride! And I am thurprithed at you, Craddock!"

"How is that?"

"I thertainly am thurprithed that you don't accuthe me of doin' thothe trickth! I thought the thilly polithe alwayth thuppothed I did everything that wath done."

"Well, you're innocent this time, Tham."

"Thankth for them kind wordth! They are thertainly apprethiated. It ith not often you are tho kind!"

"Doesn't it make you a bit mad, Tham?"

"What?"

"That somebody else is working the subway."

"Are you tryin' to inthinuate —"

"Let us drop all pretense, Tham, and put the cards on the table, faces up. You're a professional dip, and I know it; work the subway, and I know that. I'll get you if it takes me ten years. But one of you is enough! If there's another man working the subway game, I want to nab him before he gets a good start. And you don't want any competition, do you?"

"Thay! What ith the big idea? You talk a lot without thayin' much!"

"Why, I'd like to make a little arrangement with you, Tham. I want this bird, and you certainly don't want him working your game and spoiling it. If you'll scout around and locate him —"

"Thay! Are you propothin' that I turn thtool pigeon?"

"Something like that, Tham, but only to land this fellow, of course. It's as much to your interest as mine. And afterward I might turn my back — just once — and then our merry little feud will be on again."

"You make me thick! I am withe to you. I know how much you'd turn your back! There are crooked copth, but you ain't one, Craddock — I'll thay that much for you!"

"Thanks, Tham."

"Tho don't lie to me! It ith a wathte of time! And I will not be a thtool pigeon! There probably ith twenty dipth working in the thubway, and I alwayth get blamed for what all of them do!"

"So we can't make the deal?" Craddock asked.

"We thertainly can not! I thaid you wath an honetht cop, and you might thay I am an honetht crook at leatht."

"Very well, Tham. I suppose I'll have to worry along without your valuable aid. But don't get the idea for a minute that I am going to take my eyes off you."

"Thuit yourthelf!" Thubway Tham told him.

"Do you happen to be going into the subway now?"

"I happen to be goin' to eat breakfatht," Tham said.

He went down the street and turned into his favorite restaurant. Detective Craddock took up a position in front of the window to wait.

Shifty Peter watched things from across the street. This was another precaution of Thubway Tham. If another detective showed up, and Craddock turned Tham over to him, Peter would observe it and warn Tham when he came out. Tham took plenty of time about his breakfast, and then talked at length with the cashier before he went out upon the street again.

Craddock, though, was a patient man. "I'm right with you, Tham, old boy!" he said.

"Tho I thee! Closer than a silk underthirt, I thuppothe!"

"Still sarcastic, eh? I thought you'd be in a better humor after breakfast."

"With your ugly fathe in thight? That ith impothible!"

It was too early for the rush-hour crowd, and Thubway Tham walked up the street slowly, puffing at a cigarette and refusing to hold any conversation whatever with Craddock. Those were not new tactics. Tham had used them before in an effort to make Craddock so disgusted that he would cease shadowing. Craddock imagined that was what Tham was trying to do now. Tham wanted him to imagine just that, knowing that Craddock would stick close to him in such event.

For an hour, Thubway Tham prowled around the streets and finally came to Madison Square. Craddock hung on his heels, and Shifty Peter watched from across the street. Tham walked on to Twenty-eighth Street, and there he gave Shifty Peter the working sign. They went toward the subway entrance.

It was a downtown train they caught. The car was jammed with humanity. Tham stood in a corner with Craddock beside him, and Shifty Peter was near one of the doors.

"You thtill here?" Tham said to Craddock.

"I certainly am, Tham. I had begun to think that you had forgotten how to talk."

"A man mutht thpeak now and then or lothe hith voice."

"True words, Tham."

"Are you goin' to pethter me all day? The firtht thing I know, everybody will be thayin' that I am a thtool pigeon, runnin' around with you all the time."

"I fear it is necessary that I pester you, Tham."

"Can't a man have any privathy?"

"Not in the subway, Tham — not in the subway! Especially you, Tham!"

Tham was watching Shifty Peter, of course. He realized that Peter had spotted his victim, and Tham did not approve of the choice. The man was a sensitive, high-strung individual, Tham could tell at a glance, the sort of man who would know instinctively that he was being robbed. Tham tried to flash Peter a warning, but Peter was thinking of nothing now except the work in hand, and he did not even glance in Tham's direction.

Now the train was approaching the station at City Hall. Thubway Tham saw Shifty Peter move closer to his victim. Just as the train started to slow down, Tham saw Peter lurch forward, saw his hand make a lightninglike movement.

At the same instant the train stopped, the doors were opened, and Shifty Peter's victim gave a shriek and whirled around, hurling men and women right and left.

"Pickpocket! I've been robbed!" he cried.

There was instant turmoil. Craddock sprang forward. Shifty Peter had darted through the door and was already on the platform. The incoming crowd added to the confusion.

The victim shrieked again, so much that he could not reply to Craddock's questions. Shifty Peter had made good his escape by this time. Thubway Tham remained standing in the corner of the car, waiting.

Craddock made a report of the occurrence and inspected those in the car; he failed to see a known crook. The train rushed on, but before it started, Tham and Craddock had stepped out to the platform.

"Right before your thilly nothe!" Tham told him. "I thuppothe you think I did that."

"Don't be an ass, Tham. I know blamed well you didn't! But who did? That's what I want to know."

"Right on the thpot," Thubway Tham said, "and yet the man got away."

"Oh, I don't know! The fool probably lost his wallet an hour ago and just now discovered it. Believe me, boy, when I am right on the spot in a case like that, I get my man."

"Yeth?"

"Yes! And if there is another man working the subway, I'll get him — just as I am going to get you one of these days!"

They ascended to the street. Tham saw Shifty Peter a short distance away, looking very innocent and puffing at a cigarette. Tham gave him the home sign and walked down the street.

"I am goin' home to get thome retht," he told Craddock. "And I don't want to be pethered any more today."

"I'll take care of that part of it, Tham."

"Thuit yourthelf!" Tham said.

He walked down the street slowly. He came to the lodging house and entered and made sure that Craddock remained outside. He watched for ten minutes and finally saw the detective turn up the street and hurry away. The "pestering" was over for the time being. Craddock evidently had other business.

Tham hurried up to the room. Shifty Peter was waiting for him.

"Well, I got rid of the leather this time, Tham," he said.

"You are an ath!" Tham told him. "After thith, you indicate the man you have picked, and I'll let you know whether he ith all right. Anybody but a thimp would have known that wath not the thort of a man to touch."

"Well, how was I to know that he would make a noise about it?"

"Uthe your judgment, if you have any," said Tham. "After thith, you leave it to me! How much?"

"Sixty dollars."

"Thixty dollarth, and you almotht got pinched!"

"Why did you give the sign to come home so soon?"

"Great Thcott! Anybody but a thilly thimp knowth that when you are almotht caught, it ith betht to lay off for a time! It ith a thraight hunch that trouble ith lookin' your way!"

"That's bunk!" said Shifty Peter.

"Ith it? You athk any good crook. It ith not bunk!"

"Well, I didn't like the idea, Tham — coming home after turning just one trick and getting only sixty dollars."

"But it wath the only thing to do."

"You old-timers may believe in that stuff —"

"Thay! Don't call me an old-timer, Thifty! I won't thtand for it! You do ath I thay — get me? You carry out orderth and let it go at that. I know what ith betht! Grathp me?"

"Yes, I get you!"

"You'd better!" said Thubway Tham.

IV.

FOR THE following three days, Thubway Tham was trailed closely by Detective Craddock, while Shifty Peter worked on Tham's signals and lifted leathers under Craddock's nose.

Craddock was in despair. He had received a rebuke at headquarters because he had done nothing. All Craddock could say was that the man doing the work was not Thubway Tham. And so the subway was flooded with detectives and plainclothes men.

But that did no good. Thubway Tham knew them all. If there happened to be one in the car, he signaled Shifty Peter, and no leather was lifted.

These three days were prosperous ones. The sum total was almost one thousand dollars, the total having been swelled considerably by the wallet of an out-of-town buyer. Thubway Tham and Shifty Peter divided the proceeds, and Tham gave Peter a lecture on not showing sudden prosperity.

"More men have been caught that way than in any other," he said. "A man turnth a trick, and then blothomth out in glad ragth, and thpendth money on hith friendth. And along cometh thome detective to athk where all the coin came from — and then curtainth!"

"Oh, I'm not a fool, Tham!"

"No? You don't want to be, in thith buthineth! Now we'll lay off tomorrow and next day. Thothe copth are mad and there are a million of them in the thubway."

Shifty Peter smiled to his reflection in the mirror over Thubway Tham's dresser and departed. He walked around the streets for a time and sensed that inaction did not appeal to him. Thubway Tham might have been a clever man in his day, but was not Shifty Peter clever now? Tham was like an old woman, giving lectures and offering advice.

Shifty Peter decided to work alone for once. He felt confident. He felt lucky, he told himself. He would work alone, and afterward he would tell Thubway Tham and laugh at the other's advice. There was the subway, and there were people on the trains. Shifty Peter was just at the point of deciding that he was clever.

He entered the subway and rode to Times Square, and he lifted a leather. He crossed to Grand Central Station, and on the way he lifted another. He extracted the money and got rid of the purses, then went back downtown. He had been successful, and without Thubway Tham's guiding presence. He had not taken more than fifty dollars from the two wallets, but he had increased his confidence in himself, and that was the principal thing with him.

Late that afternoon, he visited Thubway Tham in his room.

"Well, I've done it!" Shifty Peter announced.

"What?"

"I failed to take your advice, Tham. I didn't see the sense of not working when there are so many people with money running around. So I went out and worked."

"You did what?"

"I went into the subway and lifted a couple of leathers. Here's your half of the swag, though you weren't working with me."

"Why, you thilly ath! You poor thimp!" Tham cried. "And maybe thome detective trailed you right here to thith room and will nab me, too."

"Oh, I guess not!"

"Thwelled in the head, are you? Then it ith all off! I thought you wath goin' to make a clever man, and I thee you are nothin' but a thwelled-head kid! Great Thcott! Don't I want coin ath much ath you do? Wouldn't I have worked with you if I had thought it would have been thafe?"

"Well, it seems to have been safe enough," Shifty Peter sneered. "You worry too much, Tham."

"I don't like it!" Tham said. "After thith, you do ath I thay! Grathp me?"

"I wanted to see you about that, too, Tham."

"What now?"

"I want to thank you for what you've taught me, of course. But I've picked up some pretty good leathers since we've been working together this way, and I've given you half of it, so I guess you ain't got any kick coming."

"What are you talkin' about?" Tham demanded.

"Well, Tham — I've decided to go into business for myself."

Thubway Tham looked at him in amazement and then got slowly out of his chair.

"Go into buthineth for yourthelf!" he said. "Why, you unthpanked kid! Goin' to leave me in the lurch, you mean? Got an idea in your head that you are thome little dip, have you? Don't care to thplit the coin any more, ith that it?"

"What's the use, when I can work alone?"

"Tho that ith the kind you are, ith it? You can't even be thquare! Go right ahead, and you'll be in jail in a week. You wath lucky today, that ith all!"

"Well, I'll take the chance, Tham. I've decided."

"How and where are you goin' to work?" Thubway Tham asked, with sudden suspicion.

"Well, in the subway, I guess."

"In the thubway? I teach you all you know, and now you want to thteal my graft?"

"You don't own the subway, do you?"

"There ith thuch a thing ath profethional honor!" Thubway Tham reminded him.

"That's more bunk!"

"Tho? Goin' to thmath all the ruleth, are you? Goin' to be a regular little double-crother? You will latht, boy, about ath long ath a piethe of ithe in a furnathe!"

"I know what I'm doing, all right!"

"But you don't!" Tham said. "You ain't got thenthe enough. You think you know all about the world and the people in it, and nobody can tell you different! I hate to thee thith! I had hopeth for you, boy, but I ain't now. Tho you are goin' to work in the thubway!"

"Don't talk rot, Tham! I guess the subway is big enough to let more than one man work in it."

"Do you know, you thimp, that every trick that ith turned in the thubway ith blamed on me?"

"Oh, so that's what's troubling you, is it?" said Shifty Peter.

"I thee there ith no uthe talkin' to a boy like you! You are goin' to be caught before you turn half a dozen trickth! You'd better not try it, boy!"

"So you'll put the cops wise to me, will you?" Shifty Peter sneered.

Thubway Tham grasped him by the throat. "You thimp!" he cried. "I ought to choke you to death! Am I a thtool pigeon? If you don't know anything about profethional honor, I do! Now you get out of here!"

He angled Shifty Peter to the door, opened it, thrust him out, then slammed the door and locked it. He shook his fists at the ceiling.

"That ith the way of it!" he said. "Never again will I try to help anybody! That thimp will get me a bad reputation! I won't be able to work until he ith caught! Well, I got money enough to live for a time. That Craddock man ith goin' to thee a lot of me in the next few dayth. I've got to be his thort of perthonal friend to have an alibi. Havin' a bull ready to thwear you are an innothent man. I gueth that ain't thome alibi!"

V.

THE FOLLOWING morning, Thubway Tham stepped from the lodging house and greeted Detective Craddock with a smile.

"Why, Tham, I am astonished!" Craddock said. "Why the joyous mood? You are positively human this morning."

"I wath jutht thinkin' that you ain't thuch a bad thport after all," Tham told him.

"That is certainly fine of you, Tham. What's the object?"

"Thir?"

"You heard me! What are you up to now?"

"I want protection, thir," Tham said.

"I don't quite get this."

"Well, there hath been conthiderable theft in the thubway of late, hath there not?"

"There has."

"And there may be more. Now, I am not goin' to be blamed for thomething I didn't do. You can watch me all you pleathe, and it will tickle me to death. I'll give you my word that I will not touch any other man's purthe thith week."

"Well, when you pass your word, you keep it; I'll say that much for you, Tham. I get you, I think. You've done enough yourself without being made to answer for what other people do."

"Thir?"

"You heard me!"

"Yeth, thir!"

"And whoever is doing all this work — we're going to land him, Tham, and make an example of him. I have an idea, from the way you act, that you know who it is."

"Great Thcott!" Tham gasped. "What maketh you think that?"

"Oh, just the way you act. If you do know, Tham, why not slip me a bit of information? The fellow is stepping on your toes, you know. How about it?"

"No, thir!"

"Very well, then, Tham! I won't urge you again. But we'll get that chap, all right, and he'll get all that is coming to him."

Craddock turned away abruptly and hurried down the street. For the time being, he feared nothing from Thubway Tham. And Tham went down the street in the other direction, toward the restaurant.

He ordered his breakfast and began eating. Shifty Peter would be nabbed before long, he felt sure; and Craddock had intimated that they would make an example of him!

To Thubway Tham there came, then, a vision of the big prison up the river. He had spent three years of his life there — and that had been a short sentence. He remembered the misery of it, the endless and monotonous days, the cruelties, the little things that break down a man's pride and self-respect until he has none left, until he is but a hulk of a human to be buffeted about the world constantly under suspicion.

Shifty Peter was but a boy. His life would be ruined. Ten years he would get — perhaps fifteen! It would break him, turn him into a beast!

Tham did not finish his breakfast. He paid his check and did not even stop to exchange words with the little cashier. He hurried from the restaurant and went down the street. He guessed where Shifty Peter could be found at this hour.

Tham found him. Already Peter was beginning to show that he was prosperous, and was laying the foundation for his own undoing. Tham called him to one side, and Peter went to him with an ingratiating smile on his lips.

"I told you yesterday that I had decided, Tham!" he said.

"Lithen! I have been talking to Craddock. Thifty, the copth are crathy! The houndth are on the trail! Boy, they are goin' to get you thure! For heaventh thake, don't do it! Do you know what a term up the river meanth? I've been there, boy! I know! I'm not thore at you for throwin' me down! I'm tryin' to thave you, boy!"

"Piffle!"

"It ith not! Can't you take an old-timer'th word for it? I don't want to thee them get a lad like you. Jutht becauthe you got the thwelled head, you want to go it alone."

"Yes, and I'm going to go it alone! This little bluff won't keep me out of your old subway, if that's what's bothering you!"

"It ith not that —"

"Bunk!" said Shifty Peter. He swung around and left Thubway Tham standing there.

Tham regained the street and stood on the corner. He felt a certain amount of anger, of course, yet he felt sorry for Peter. He felt some responsibility in the affair, for he had taught the boy, had suggested the career to him, in fact.

Tham waited across the street until half an hour later, when Peter came out and started toward the nearest subway entrance. Thubway Tham shadowed him as cleverly as any detective ever shadowed a suspect. He followed him to the platform, into the train. He glanced quickly around the car, saw a detective he knew, nodded to him, and moved over closer to him. He wanted the officer to be able to say, afterward, that Thubway Tham could not have done it.

As he talked, he watched Shifty Peter. He saw Peter select his victim. Tham approved of the selection. He watched Peter step nearer as the train approached a station. Peter was working after Thubway Tham's own manner.

He saw the quick move of Peter's hand — and then there was a sudden turmoil. The victim had thrown back his own hand just in time to encounter Peter's and had voiced his anger and surprise in no uncertain tones.

Peter had managed to step back half a dozen feet — but he had the loot in his pocket! Thubway Tham could tell by the expression in the boy's face that he was terrified, that he had lost his nerve for the moment, when he needed it most. He had forgotten all that Thubway Tham had told him to do in case of such an emergency.

The detective had sprung forward, and Tham darted after him. He knew that, when they reached the station, a search would be made of everybody in that car. He reached Peter's side, his hand darted down and took the wallet from Peter's pocket. The boy, suddenly remembering, thanked him with his eyes.

Then Thubway Tham lunged forward again. Once more his hand made a quick movement.

Back in the crowd again, Thubway Tham waited patiently for the searching process. Peter had had sense enough to get away from his vicinity. The detective called other officers at the station, and the men were searched well. They frisked Shifty Peter and found nothing. Finally they turned to Thubway Tham.

"Oh, I didn't get it!" Tham said. "I wath talkin' to the bull when it happened."

"You'll stand a search, just the same!" they told him.

There was an expression of horror in the face of Shifty Peter. They would find the wallet on Tham, he supposed. Tham would be sent up the river for something he had not done. Poor old Thubway Tham! And he, a headstrong boy, would be the cause of it!

His eyes widened. They had ended their search of Tham and had discovered nothing. They found no stolen wallet on anybody in the car. They opened the doors, and the passengers stepped to the platform and went up to the street.

Shifty Peter followed Thubway Tham dumbly. Four blocks down the street, he stepped alongside.

"Thanks, Tham — thanks!" he whispered. "You saved me, Tham! My nerve was gone for a moment. And, Tham, I don't want to work alone any more."

"We'll talk it over later, boy."

"But where did that wallet go?"

"Why, you thilly ath! I knew that they would thearch everybody in that car. You didn't think I would keep it and let them find it on me, did you?"

"But they didn't find it on anybody else!"

"Thertainly not! That detective never thearched himthelf, did he? I knew he wouldn't. Tho I jutht dropped that wallet in the detective'th pocket. Thee? When he findth it there, he will be one thurprithed cop!"

And Thubway Tham walked on down the street, while Shifty Peter, his conceit gone, looked after him in wonder.

THUBWAY THAM'S BAGGAGE CHECK

HE sat in one corner of the smoking compartment of the Pullman car, next to the window, and watched the flying landscape closely. In one hand he held a railroad time-table, and he glanced at it, and at his watch, as each station was passed. If the limited was on time, very well and good; but, if it happened to be a couple of minutes late at any particular point, he acted as if about to go in search of the conductor and demand an immediate explanation.

For he was going home!

He was a little man, and apparently nervous to a great degree. His nostrils were thin, and his eyes furtive, and it seemed that his fingers were continually moving. Those same fingers were clever, though the other men in the smoking room did not guess it. Those fingers had been trained through the years, to explore foreign pockets quickly and without discovery.

But their owner had no intention of making them do their regular work now. The men in the smoking room with him, even had they been aware of his identity and reputation, could have continued their journeys without fear, and without keeping their hands on their wallets and watches continually. Those fingers, as a usual thing, did their nefarious work only in a certain small section of the vast country — a section toward which the limited now was rushing.

The little man who sat next the window in the smoking room had almost fought at Chicago to get an upper berth in an extra-fare train. He wanted to get to New York as quickly as possible, he had explained, hinting that it was a matter of life and death or something like that and even the extra-fare limited would be too slow. He had obtained the reservation — and now he sat at the window and watched the stations and the time-table, and fumed and fussed.

He made no attempt to hold a conversation with any of the other passengers in the smoking room, and if a man addressed him he got only a grunt by way of reply. The little man sitting next the window appeared to be occupied with his thoughts — which was exactly the case.

Down the river rushed the train, through city after city, devouring the miles with a speed that was amazing. Now it passed within a short distance of a great gray prison, whereupon the little man sitting next the window seemed to be trying to make himself yet smaller, and he almost closed his eyes. He knew that prison well — he had spent a terrible three years there some time before. He shuddered at the memory of those three years.

He watched the sparkling river through the window. He began to notice things that he recognized and knew. His heart was warming gradually. He was getting home!

He had been away with the exception of one flying visit to the city, for a little more than a year, had been to the Pacific coast, had spent the greater part of the time in southern California, where the warm sunshine and soft sea breezes had done much for him.

He had been glad to make the journey to the Western country, for the state of his health had demanded an instant change of climate — and there had been other important reasons. But recently the great city on the Hudson had been calling him again, and finally he had packed his trunk and had answered the call.

The train was entering the outskirts of the city now, and the little man sat up straighter in his seat and betrayed a sudden interest. This was New York! This was home! She had her faults, but in all the world there was no other city like her! She could be cruel, and she could be kind. She was vast in some things, and small in others.

The little man left the smoking room and went into the car. He stopped beside his seat, put on his coat and hat and picked up his traveling bag.

"You gettin' off at Hundred an' Twenty-fifth?" the porter asked.

"I am!" the little man grunted.

The porter took the bag and started toward the end of the car, and the little man followed. He did not care to continue downtown to the Grand Central Terminal. He was not eager to have certain persons know that he had returned to the city — at least not until he had had an opportunity to see how things were going and learn any news that might have a peculiar interest for him. And at the Grand Central Terminal, he knew, there might be certain men who would recognize him instantly, and draw their own conclusions.

When the train stopped at the uptown station, he dropped off, hurried to the street; and walked along it rapidly for a distance of a few blocks. He came to a subway station — and stopped.

He dropped the bag to the walk and wiped the perspiration from his forehead. He looked around at the people and the signs and the buildings and at the subway station again. And then he grinned after the manner of a man who is well pleased.

"Thame old thubway!" he exclaimed. "Thame old plathe! It thertainly lookth good to me!"

And so Thubway Tham —

What? You didn't guess that it was Thubway Tham?

You know Thubway Tham, of course, the clever little pickpocket who worked only in the subway during rush hours — so clever that a city detective had been assigned especially to trail him. You remember, perhaps, how Thubway Tham outwitted certain gentlemen with considerable profit to himself — one of the gentlemen being Craddock, the detective mentioned — and then went West for his health?

Now he had returned, benefited in every way, refreshed and more clever than before, his wits on keener edge. He stood before the subway station, and his nostrils opened wide to drink in the breath of the big tube he loved.

Thubway Tham was home!

He stood on the corner for as much as ten minutes, just enjoying the scene. Then he picked up his traveling bag, and hurried forward to purchase a ticket and start downtown.

II.

THUBWAY THAM did not go to the rooming house where he formerly had lived. He knew that the place was under police surveillance, and he did not care, just at present, to let Craddock, his old enemy, know that he had returned.

He went to a small, respectable place and obtained a room. He ate a meal at an obscure restaurant, purchased the evening newspapers, and returned to his room to investigate the news.

He found something to interest him on the front page of his favorite journal. The article said that a certain broker of prominence, traveling in the subway because of a broken motor car, had been relieved of a wallet containing a large sum of money. The police, the article said, were of the opinion that there was a new subway pickpocket at work. They hinted that formerly there had been a famous pickpocket who worked in the subway, but that he had been out of the city for several months, hence could not be guilty of this latest crime. And there had been minor robberies recently, too, the newspaper said.

"Thome thilly thimp!" Thubway Tham told himself. "Playin' my game, ith he?"

And then a thought came to Thubway Tham. He was believed to be out of the city. The detectives were searching for a new man — they were not looking for Thubway Tham. Why could not Thubway Tham do his work and let this new man, who had invaded a precinct sacred to Tham, take the blame for all the crimes? He could do it, Tham decided, as long as he kept from Craddock and others on the police force the knowledge that he had returned to the city.

Tham considered the matter throughout the evening, remaining in his room. He had told the landlord that he had just arrived from a long journey, was tired, and needed a long sleep. Tham realized that his appearance was not much altered, except that his cheeks were fuller and had a better color, and his hair was longer. His clothes were different, of course, but he couldn't place much faith in that fact. There was a slight risk he would have to run. He arose at an early hour the following morning, and after eating breakfast wandered around the streets, making friends with the great city again. He did not visit any of his old haunts, however, and he was alert for detectives who might recognize him. He wanted to see and talk to his old friends, but he knew that it would not do at present.

Word soon would be spread around town that Thubway Tham had

returned, and it would reach the ears of the police, and Craddock.

Tham wondered a great deal about Craddock. There had been quite a fight between them in the old days — a game of wits in which Tham always had emerged the victor. Craddock had sworn to "get him," but Craddock fought fair, at least.

"The old thilly ath!" Thubway Tham told himself. "Like to get a look at him jutht to thee how he ith lookin'."

The rush hour came, and Thubway Tham descended into the subway at City Hall and started northward. He left the train at Times Square, and he took a fat wallet with him. Tham was glad to find that his fingers had not lost their cunning. He had been away for a year, and he had not worked at his "trade" during that time.

He boarded a train for downtown, and managed to get another wallet. He disposed of the "leathers" quickly, keeping only currency; which is very difficult to identify, especially if the bills are of small denominations.

He went back to Times Square, boarded the shuttle train, journeyed to Grand Central in the midst of the throng, returned, and lifted another wallet. Next he made the trip downtown again, went to his room, and found that the day's work had netted him a profit of about three hundred dollars. It was a far larger profit than usual. Thubway Tham considered it a good omen.

The morning newspapers were filled with articles about the carnival of crime in the subway, and certain detectives received orders that something had to be done or there would be divers and sundry transfers and things like that.

Once more, Thubway Tham worked at rush hour. He worked carefully, yet desperately. In the old days he had been content to lift one wallet, or perhaps two at the most, but that was when Craddock was trailing him most of the time and he was obliged to work beneath the nose of the detective.

Now he lifted wallets as rapidly as possible, for he wanted to maintain the carnival of crime. Reports poured into police headquarters, and a superior officer in the detective department sent for Craddock.

"Something funny about this subway business," he said.

"It's either a new man — or a gang," Craddock replied.

"Looks like a gang, the number of reports we've been getting. How about Thubway Tham?"

"Still out of town," Craddock said. "I got to thinking about him, too. I've trailed around his old hangouts, but haven't found a trace of him. Been expecting him to come back about this time, and have been watching for him. If he was back, he'd show himself right away. He'd think it was smart to dare me to catch him."

"Well, get busy!" Craddock's superior warned him. "I don't like this chorus of howls. We've got to land somebody, and do it mighty quick. Get busy!"

Craddock and his associates got busy. They haunted the subway from one end of it to the other. They rode back and forth until they began to hate the underground railroad, yet they caught no pickpockets, either male or female.

Thubway Tham, reading the newspapers carefully, knew that he was not the only man working in the subway. There were reported robberies of which he had not been guilty. Wherefore rage was born within him.

In the old days, before he had gone west, it had been understood in the underworld that Thubway Tham's district was the big tube, and other dips refrained from working there. Once a man had tried it, and Thubway Tham had punished him. Here was somebody trying it now.

But Tham was honest in his way. He had not let it be known in the underworld that he had returned, and so he could not exactly blame the man who was working in his district. He was not ready yet to let anybody know he was in the city.

For a week, he worked during the rush hours. He obtained many wallets, and at the same time he watched for the other man, but never located him. Tham was piling up money, but he knew that it could not go on. Half a dozen times he had narrowly escaped being seen by an officer who knew him. And, if he was recognized, the people at headquarters might blame all the recent subway work on him!

"I thuppothe I'll have to let 'em know that I am in the thity thoon," Tham told himself one evening. "Then that ath of a Craddock will be on my trail. He'll pethter the life out of me! There ith no uthe talkin' —

thometimeth that man maketh me thick!"

The following day, he saw Craddock at a distance, but managed to prevent himself being observed by the detective. And, half an hour later, on an express train approaching Fourteenth Street, Thubway Tham found his rival.

He saw the man do his work — take a wallet from a fat individual who carried it in his hip pocket. When the dip left the train, Tham followed. The other man was tall and broad-shouldered, and did not look at all like the ordinary pickpocket, a fact that probably had saved him from arrest, he had the appearance of an ordinary business man.

"Thilly ath!" Tham said. "Workin' my game, ith he? I'll get thquare with him!"

He followed his rival into the subway again at another station, watched him lift another leather, and edge forward. Tham waited his chance, until the other was about to leave the train at a crowded platform. His hand made a lightninglike movement — and Tham had the wallet the other man had stolen. He remained on the train as his rival left, and he was smiling.

That night, as he sat in his room, he began considering that it perhaps would be better, now, to visit his old haunts. If Craddock met him, and learned that he had been in the city for some days, the detective would believe he had been hard at work. Tham wanted Craddock to keep on looking for a criminal who was a stranger. He even wanted Craddock to take that stranger into custody after a time, for Tham felt sure that the other man was an outsider who had no business robbing the people of New York.

On the following day, Tham went forth as usual, alert for officers of the law, ready to dodge any old friend he might see, eager to make a last haul before announcing his presence in the city.

He boarded a train at Union Square and started uptown. At the next station, he saw his rival get aboard.

Thubway Tham had noticed a prosperous-looking gentleman standing near one end of the car, and had speculated on removing valuables from the gentleman's pocket. But now he watched his rival.

The tall man glanced at the others in the car, and he, too, saw the prosperous-looking individual. Thubway Tham realized that the other had picked this man for a victim, and he felt his anger gathering again. With all the subway trains, and with all the persons riding on them, was it at all necessary for this interloper to pick the man that Tham himself had decided to rob?

"Maketh me thick!" Tham growled low down in his throat.

He decided to allow the tall man to work his will. Something like a hunch had come to Thubway Tham. He had a feeling of uneasiness. There seemed to be disaster in the air. He made his way toward the other end of the car, but got into a position from which he could watch the other.

The train was approaching a station. Tham saw the other man's hand make a familiar move, and turned away. Instantly he turned back again — for to his ears had come a screech of rage.

The rival pickpocket had bungled. His victim had caught him in the act. Now they were scuffling at the other end of the car. Thubway Tham saw that the tall man could not get rid of the wallet he had taken. And then another man took a hand in the game — a broad-shouldered, black-mustached man Tham knew instantly for an officer working in plain clothes.

The train stopped at the station, and officer, prisoner and victim got off. Tham rode to the next station and then returned downtown by means of the back streets. The thing had unnerved him to a degree.

III.

THUBWAY THAM did no work for the following week, and he spent a great deal of time in his room. The papers announced the capture of the pickpocket, and that the carnival of crime in the subway apparently had come to an end. That was what Thubway Tham wanted. He grinned when be read that the prisoner disclaimed knowledge of more than half the recent robberies. The police did not believe him, of course, especially since the crimes had ceased with his arrest.

At the end of the week, Tham considered that it now would be safe for him to enter the city officially and make his presence known. That would be the best way, he knew. He could not hope to hide, and if caught doing it, he merely would cause Craddock and the others to suspect him and watch him more than usual.

He went far uptown one morning, and for a time walked around Central Park. It was his last chance for some time, he knew. Craddock had told him more than a year and a half before that his presence in that section of the city would mean instant arrest on a vagrancy charge. Men of Thubway Tham's ilk knew better than to invade certain parts of the metropolis.

He sat down on a bench behind a clump of brush, in a secluded part of the park, and gave himself up to meditation. After a time, voices reached his ears, and he realized that two men were on the other side of the clump of brush, and that they were speaking in low tones.

Thubway Tham parted the bushes and observed them. They were well dressed and appeared to be persons of prominence, but Tham knew instantly that they were not honest men.

"Amateur crookth," he told himself.

Tham hated an amateur crook. The underworld hated them. Genuine crooks, who knew the ethics of their calling, were all right. They played the game, and if they were caught they paid the penalty. Either a crook or an honest man, but not an attempt to be both, said the underworld.

Thubway Tham grew interested in the conversation he heard, and in what he saw. One of the men opened a traveling bag he had, took several packages of bills from his pocket and put them into the bag. The other watched for anybody to approach.

"Now we'll go to the Grand Central and check this bag," one of the men was saying. "That's the safest thing in the world. We'll leave it there until the investigation is over at the office. When we are sure that they do not suspect us, we'll merely take down the check, pay the storage bill, and catch a train."

There was considerable more talk, and Thubway Tham drank it in. It appeared that these men had robbed an employer who believed them to be faithful. They had worked for him for years; and had decided to take all they could at one time and depart for other scenes.

"Why, the dirty crookth!" Thubway Tham told himself.

The men walked on through the park, and Tham followed them at a distance. Had these been genuine, professional crooks, he would have turned away from them, but an amateur crook was to be despised and taught the error of his ways when possible.

Tham followed them to the nearest subway entrance, and got on a train behind them. He was alert for sight of an officer, glad that he saw none. The Grand Central was dangerous territory, he knew. There always were detectives prowling around the big station.

The men went to the check stand, and one of them checked the bag and put the pasteboard into a pocket of his waistcoat. Then they left the station and started walking along Forty-second Street.

Thubway Tham trailed them through the crowds, trying to keep them in sight constantly and dodge officers at the same time. Now and then he got near enough to realize that they were maintaining a conversation, but he could not distinguish their words.

He followed them to Times Square and down into the subway. They boarded an express for downtown, and Thubway Tham got into the same car with them.

Tham wanted that check, but taking a thing like that from a waistcoat pocket is dangerous and requires a maximum of skill. Assured that no officer he knew was in the car, he worked near the two men, who were standing, and finally was pressing against the one who had the check.

Thubway Tham began to despair. He watched for an opportunity, but none presented itself. Then accident came to his aid.

At one end of the car, one man stepped upon the foot of another. The apology was not accepted, and hot words followed. There was a sudden commotion as fisticuffs started, and the man who had the check in his pocket stretched his neck and bent his head to see the row. Thubway Tham's hand did its work, and the check was in his possession.

He left the train at the next station, and immediately caught another uptown. He reached Times Square, took the shuttle to Grand Central, and hurried toward the parcel check stand. And then he saw his old enemy, Detective Craddock.

Tham dodged behind half a dozen persons who were crowding forward to the stand. He saw another detective, and dodged back. Craddock caught sight of him, hurried toward him.

"Well, well, if it isn't my old friend Tham!" Craddock said.

Tham regarded him with scorn. "By heaventh!" said Tham. "I no thooner get back to town than I am pethtered with the thight of your homely fathe! I went away and thtayed a whole year jutht to forget your ugly mug, and here you are waitin' when I come back."

"Just in from the Golden West, eh?"

"The Wetht may be golden, but little old New York ith good enough for me," Tham said.

"Well, I suppose you'll be up to your old tricks again, Tham," Craddock told him. "I suppose I'll have to trail you as I did before, to keep you from bothering gentlemen with wallets."

"Thay! Jutht becauthe I onthe wath thent up —"

"Now, please don't begin that, Tham. Don't start any of that 'give a dog a bad name' stuff on me. I'm wise to you, Tham, all right, and don't you forget it!"

"Withe? You?" Thubway Tham sneered. "If you are withe, I mutht be King Tholomon himthelf. If you are withe I am a college profethor. If you are withe —"

"Pray, cease!" Craddock said. "When did you get in?"

"Thith morning," Tham replied, remembering that there was a morning train from Chicago that was a favorite with the traveling public.

"Sure of that?"

"Of courthe. Why?"

"Tham, somebody has been working your beat."

"What do you mean by that?" Tham demanded.

"I mean that, up to a week or so ago, some gent has been bothering persons in the old subway. He picked pockets right and left and center, Tham. But we got him."

"Tho?"

"Caught him with the goods, Tham; and that's what we're going to do to you one of these days if you don't change your mode of life. And this particular crook declares he didn't commit half those crimes Tham. Some of them seemed a lot like your work. If I thought you had been in town any length of time, I'd just take you up to talk to the captain about it."

"Well, my grathiouth!" Tham exclaimed. "I don't any more than get off the train before I am accuthed of thomething! Before I get a chance to rent me a room —"

"You're quite sure you just got in this morning, Tham?"

"Ofcourthe!"

"And you haven't rented a room yet?"

"No. I am going to my old plathe, if you want to know."

"Then, where is your bag?" Craddock demanded, pointing a finger at him.

Thubway Tham gulped. He had been afraid of that question, but he was ready for it.

"In the check thtand," he replied. "Here ith the check. Thee? You make me thick, Craddock!"

Thubway Tham turned his back, went to the stand, and handed in the check. To say that he felt no fear would be to write a falsehood. He was desperately afraid that Craddock would insist that he open the bag. And how could he, when he had no key for it? If it was opened, how could he explain those packages of money and the other articles?

He was glad that his back was turned toward Craddock, for it gave him time to compose himself. The bag was handed to him, and he whirled around again, a smile on his face.

"It ith good to be back, even if your ugly fathe ith the firtht I thee," Thubway Tham said. "Will you hold thith bag, Craddock, while I light a thigarette?"

Detective Craddock would, and did. He carried the bag, moreover, as they walked to the main entrance, for it seemed that Thubway Tham had trouble with his matches.

"Going to use the subway?" Craddock asked.

"Ofcourthe!"

"Um! I guess I'll just ride a part of the way with you, Tham."

"Go ath far ath you like," Tham told him. "We thtrive to pleathe. I am goin' to get my old room if I can, and then —"

"And then you'll be up to your old tricks, eh?"

"Maybe you had better wait," Tham said angrily. "Maybe you had better wait until I do thomething to give you cauthe to talk that way to me. You make me thick, Craddock! Give me that bag!"

Tham took it from him and led the way down the street.

"Why not take the subway from Grand Central?" Craddock asked.

"Well, by heathenth! I have been away for more than a year, and I want to thee the old town!" Tham replied. "I am going to walk to Timeth Thquare and take a train there."

"Well, I'll not pester you just now, Tham," Craddock said. "But I'll be watching you, old boy. And one of these days I'll nab you, and get you right. Then it will be up the river for yours."

"Tho? When that day cometh, it will mean that I am thlowin' up," Tham said. "You couldn't catch a cold, Craddock. Thankth, however, for not pethterin' me today."

"Don't mention it, Tham."

"And thankth, altho, for carryin' my bag," Thubway Tham added. "You are very kind. Thith ith a good bag."

"And you've probably got one shirt, a couple of collars and a pair of socks in it, even if you do happen to have a good front," Craddock said, laughing.

"Perhapth," said Tham. "A man mutht run a bluff onthe in a while, muthn't he? He muth!"

And Thubway Tham, now in the city officially, and safe for the present, hurried on up the street. When he had gone half a block and was sure that Craddock was not following, he began, to chuckle.

"The thilly ath!" he said. "Right under hith nothe!"

THUBWAY THAM, PHILANTHROPIST

"THOME highbrow onthe thaid that it ith the thingth right under our nothe that we never thee. The uthual man, thaid he, ith farthighted. Becauthe of that, a man lookth at thingth far away and, ath a rethult, tripth over thingth that are right under hith feet. He altho mitheth a lot of interething thingth. Which only goeth to thow that the uthual man ith a thilly ath."

Standing before the cracked mirror in the dilapidated dresser in his room at the cheap lodging house, making the appropriate gestures, this sentiment was delivered into the ether for the benefit of the world at large by no less a person than Thubway Tham.

You know Tham, of course. He was a pickpocket, and he worked only in the subway during rush hours, and he lisped, and thereby earned his name, which was an honored one in the underworld.

Thubway Tham recently had returned after a year spent in southern California, where he had gone because of ill health, and because, also, certain officers of the law, particularly a detective named Craddock, were making things unpleasant for him.

He was quartered in the same lodging house where he had had a room before his journey — a greasy, ramshackle lodging house on a certain side street, operated by a man formerly a crook and a convict. The statement goes double — the same man operated the lodging house and the street.

Craddock knew that Thubway Tham was in the city, of course, for Tham had found it necessary to visit his old haunts and look up his friends. The detective had repeated his threat to get Tham "with the goods" and send him to the big prison up the river. Thubway Tham, hearing that oft-repeated boast, had placed his thumb against his nose and had extended his fingers in a gesture known throughout the world. The gesture meant that Detective Craddock could betake himself to a realm where it is warm.

Tham had refrained from invading the subway and "lifting leathers" for a few days. In the first place, he was in funds for the time being; in the second place, he wanted to rest a bit; and, in the third place, he wanted Detective Craddock to get over his present eagerness. For Craddock was no fool. He was a worthy foe, and on numerous occasions he had come so near to undoing Thubway Tham that Tham felt shivers playing up and down his spinal column.

Not being engaged in his usual nefarious pursuit, Thubway Tham had time to look around. There were certain sections of the city where his presence was not desired by officers of the law, and so Thubway Tham had to content himself with explorations "below the line."

Thus it occurred that he came upon a certain thing in the alley back of the lodging house where he lived, and within fifty feet of the side door that Thubway Tham had used many times.

Walking through the alley because it was a short cut to a certain restaurant, Thubway Tham had seen a shack. It was propped between the back of two buildings, and looked as if it would have been unable to stand alone. Tham thought at first that it was a storehouse of some sort, but as the door was open and he happened to glance inside, he made the discovery that it was a human habitation.

That startled Thubway Tham. He knew the sordid and seamy side of life, but he was not aware of the fact that human beings lived in a sort of rundown doghouse like that. He went to the restaurant and returned by way of the alley, his curiosity aroused. When he returned, he found an old man sitting on a soap box before the door of the shack.

"You live here?" Thubway Tham asked.

"I do," said the old man. Thubway Tham looked at him closely. He was a very old man, it was evident at a first glance. He had long hair and an unkempt beard, and they would have been white had they been clean. As it was, they had a color all their own. The old man's clothing consisted of greasy garments in rags. There was a hungry look in the old man's face, and his hands shook.

"Alone?" asked Thubway Tham.

"Me and my ole woman," said the man.

Thubway Tham felt a shock go through him. It was bad enough for a man to live in such a place, infinitely worse for an old man — but an old woman —

"My heaventh!" Thubway Tham gasped.

He walked closer to the old man and lighted a cigarette. He puffed at it and regarded the other intently.

"That ith tough," Tham said.

"Eh?" asked the old man.

"Can't you live in a better place than thith?"

"Can't afford it!"

"Ith your wife in good health?"

The old man sighed.

"She's in misery all the time," he said. "She suffers quite a lot on account of pains in her back and legs. Rheumatism, I reckon. She's had it for years."

"It doeth not thurprithe me any," Tham told him. "Livin' in a plathe like thith —"

"We never had any luck," the old man said. "And now I ain't able to do a stroke of work, nor my ole woman, either. We just manage to keep the wolf from the door, and sometimes he gets near enough at that for us to hear him sniffin'. It's a terrible thing for old people to hear the wolf sniffin'; yep, I reckon it is."

"My heaventh!" Tham gasped again.

"I've got a license to play a hand-organ, but I don't make much. The organ ain't in tune, and my hands shake so I can't hardly play her. But we manage to get along some way. Ah, well, it won't be for long now."

"Well, ain't there thome plathe for folkth like you?" Thubway Tham wanted to know. "Ain't there any hometh rich men have built for old folkth that can't manage to get along good?"

"Fakes!" the old man explained. "I tried every way to get into one of them with the ole woman, but they wouldn't have none of us. Politics, I reckon. They're down on me. Years ago there was a certain election when I didn't vote right, and they've never forgotten it. Nope!"

"Well, my goodneth! The thkunkth!" said Thubway Tham.

The old man bowed his head and brushed away a tear. Thubway

Tham felt a sudden lump in his throat. He blinked his eyes and looked down the alley.

"Well, I've got to be goin'," he told the old man. "Maybe I'll thee you again thome day!"

Tham went to the lodging house and up the stairs to his own room. The sight of the poverty-stricken patriarch had pained him. He hated to think of an old man and his aged wife living in such squalor. Thubway Tham was a pickpocket and had served time, but he had a tender heart.

"It ith up to me," Tham told himself.

He settled it in exactly that manner. He had decided to be a philanthropist. And then it was that he delivered his oration to the effect that there are things right under our noses that we never see because we are always viewing things in the distance.

II.

THE FOLLOWING day Thubway Tham prepared himself for work. He had decided not to labor for a month, at least, but he found it necessary now. He wanted to help the old man who lived in the shack, and there was only one way to do it.

Tham had no intention of playing philanthropist with his own money. The old man had said that the rich and the powerful were against him, and so Tham decided that the rich and powerful should pay. He would go into his beloved subway, and he would purloin a wallet belonging to somebody who appeared to be rich and powerful, and with the contents of that wallet he would purchase supplies for the old man and his aged wife.

Tham also had decided to make the charity anonymous. In the first place, he could not endure to be thanked for anything, and, besides, he did not care to have investigating police officers learn that he had so much money that he was aiding the poor. They might want to know where he got it.

His heart singing in anticipation of his good deed, Thubway Tham left the lodging house and went to the usual restaurant for breakfast. Then he made his way toward the north, smoking a cigarette and walking slowly, for it was not yet the hour when New Yorkers stampede in the subway and make the work of a pickpocket easy. The rush hour appealed strongly to Thubway Tham.

At a certain corner somebody slapped Tham on his back, and he whirled around to see Detective Craddock's smiling face.

"Good morning, Tham," the detective said.

"It ith not a good morning when I thee your ugly fathe," Tham said. "I have told you that theveral timeth. Are you goin' to pethter the life out of me thith mornin'?"

"Those who live by the sword, Tham, shall die by the sword," Craddock said.

"Now, what thenthe ith there in that?" Tham demanded.

"You grasp me all right, Tham. A gentleman of your profession should expect to have a detective keep an eye on him now and then."

"My goodneth! Are you a detective?" Tham asked.

"So they say, Tham — so they say."

"You thertainly are puttin' thomething over on thomebody," Tham told him. "Do you draw a thalary and everythin'?"

"I get my regular stipend, Tham."

"The poor taxpayerth!" Tham gasped.

"Putting aside all jokes, Tham, are you contemplating a trip in our beautiful subway today?"

"Why do you athk?"

"I am interested in a measure, Tham. I have noticed that whenever you take a ride in the subway there come a complaint into headquarters an hour or so later about a missing purse."

"Ath if I cared," Tham said.

"And, putting two and two together, Tham — you understand, I trust?"

"Thay! Jutht becauthe I onthe wath —"

"Don't say it, Tham. I know that piece by heart. Just because you once made a slip and were caught, the police should not take it to mean that you are a habitual criminal, eh?"

"Give a dog a bad name —"

"Oh, I understand. But don't try that line of talk on me. Put on a new record when I am visiting with you, Tham. That one grows stale. I wasn't born yesterday."

"No?"

"No!" said Craddock. "And, if you are going to take a ride in the subway, I'm going right along."

"The thubway needth the money," Tham told him. "I thuppothe you'll put it on your expenthe account."

"You said it, Tham."

Tham did not reply. He glared at Craddock, and then he turned his back deliberately and walked up the street. He reached Union Square and went into the subway entrance, knowing that Craddock was but a step behind him.

Boarding an uptown train, Tham journeyed as far as Times Square, and there he started downtown again and went to Pearl Street. Once more he went uptown to Times Square, took the shuttle train and crossed to the Grand Central terminal, and from there went downtown again. Craddock stepped up to him as Tham reached the street.

"Are you doing this for exercise, Tham?" he asked.

"Jutht killin' time," Tham said. "The thubway needth the money."

"You mean you're killing time until the rush hour crowds get on the trains," Craddock accused him.

"I'm killin' time until you get through pethterin' me. I am goin' to thee your both about thith. I hate to thee a detective wathte hith time."

"Wasting my time, am I?" Craddock asked.

"You thertainly are," said Tham. "Why don't you trail thome crook?"

"I am."

Tham's face flushed, and, for an instant, anger flashed in his eyes.

"Even if you are," said Tham, "you are wathting your time. If I wanted to lift a leather I could do it right under your thilly nothe and you'd never know it."

"Yes?"

"Yeth! Ath a detective, you are a fine butcher," Tham told him. "You thpoil all the joy in life. You make me thick! In my ethtimation you are a thimp!"

"Harsh words, Tham — very harsh words."

"If I can think up any thtronger oneth, I'll tell them to you," Tham retorted.

He turned his back again and walked up the street, and again Detective Craddock followed at his heels. Tham used the subway once more, and left it at City Hall. He had timed his arrival correctly. The streets were thronged. Tham leaned against the front of a building and watched the crowds.

Craddock began to get nervous. He moved away, and he walked back, but Thubway Tham made no attempt to dodge him. Finally, in huge disgust he went to the corner, and around it.

Tham saw him go. But he waited for several minutes, puffing at his cigarette and watching the crowds. Then he turned suddenly and darted into the building against which he had been standing, hurried through it, and emerged on the side street. Two minutes later, he was in the subway, and Craddock was off the trail.

Tham boarded an uptown train and looked about the car. He made sure first that there was no officer he knew in that car. And then he looked for a victim.

He saw one immediately — a prosperous-looking man who stood near one of the doors. Thubway Tham edged toward the man and got in the proper position. He brushed against him, and made certain that his intended victim carried a wallet in one of his hip pockets. Thubway Tham always had declared that a man fool enough to carry a wallet there should be robbed and taught a lesson.

Getting the wallet was not difficult. Tham accomplished it just as the train stopped at a station, got off and hurried to the street, removed the bills the wallet contained, and thrust them into a pocket of his waistcoat, then dropped the wallet itself into the first trash can he came across. There was no evidence on him now, for the wallet was gone and currency is difficult to identify unless the bills are of large denomination or have been marked.

Tham journeyed downtown again, spent the remainder of the afternoon in peaceful pursuits, and as evening approached went to a grocery and market. He purchased a huge basket and had it filled with provisions. Meats, vegetables, canned goods, butter, eggs, milk — Tham purchased them all, and in large quantities. Then he carried the basket to his room.

There he got an envelope, and into it he put the last few bills that he had taken from the stolen wallet and had not spent. He slipped the envelope into one end of the basket.

"Not a thent of profit," Thubway Tham told himself. "Thith ith jutht a good deed — that ith all! That old man and hith wife are goin' to have thingth to eat!"

Tham waited until about an hour after nightfall, then slipped quietly down the rear stairs and went into the alley. A cracked shade hung over the one window of the shack. Tham could see through one of the cracks.

He saw the old man and his aged wife. The man was reading a newspaper that looked as if it had been recovered from a trash can, and his wife was darning a shabby shawl.

"It ith a thame," Tham told himself. "That ith no way for folkth to live."

He put the basket in front of the door and knocked. Then he darted silently down the alley, and from a distance, watched the old man open the door, stumble over the basket, pick it up, and carry it into the shack.

Thubway Tham had pleasant dreams that night.

III.

THE FOLLOWING morning Tham walked through the alley on his way to the restaurant and found the old man sitting in the doorway of the shack.

"How do you feel thith mornin'?" Tham asked him.

"A trifle better," the old man replied. "Some Good Samaritan was kind to me last night."

"How wath that?"

"Somebody left a basket of provisions on the step," the old man said. "Some kind soul knows that we are in need, I reckon."

"Well, ain't that nithe!" Tham said. "So you had thomething to eat?"

"Big basket full," said the old man. "But the ole woman and me ain't wasteful at all. I took the meat — a big roast it was — and sold it back to the butcher and got some salt pork with the money. It won't spoil, it'll last longer, and that's economy. Yes, sir."

"My goodneth!" Tham exclaimed.

"I sold back some of the canned goods, too, and the basket," the old man said.

"Thee here!" Tham broke in. "You don't want to do that. If thomebody gave you that thtuff they meant for you to eat it. You and your wife would not be thick if you'd eat better thtuff."

"But I don't like to be wasteful," said the old man. "My ole woman and me ain't used to fancy grub like that."

"Well, get uthed to it!" Tham told him. "Maybe you'll be gettin' more."

"No, I reckon not. Lightnin' don't strike twice in the same place," the old man told him. "Like as not, somebody made a mistake when they put that basket of grub there."

Thubway Tham chuckled as he went on through the alley. He promised himself that he'd continue to leave provisions and money at the door of the shack until the old man and his wife grew accustomed to the idea and began living properly. Clothing, too, would not be amiss, Tham told himself. He made an attempt to dodge Craddock that day, but the detective picked him up in the vicinity of Union Square. It taxed Tham's ingenuity to evade the officer, but he accomplished it after a time, and finally succeeded in purloining a wallet from a gentleman who had the appearance of being a malefactor of great wealth.

Tham was gratified to find that the wallet contained eighty dollars. He purchased another basket that evening, and had it filled with provisions, and he bought an overcoat for the old man and a new shawl for his aged wife. Cold weather was approaching.

Once more, after night had fallen, Thubway Tham crept down the lodging house stairs and went into the alley, and once more he stood at a distance and watched the old man take in the basket.

"Hope he keepth the thtuff thith time," Tham told himself. "He thertainly doeth need a thquare meal!"

IT WAS almost noon the day following when Tham went through the alley and found the old man sitting in the doorway.

"Feeling better thith mornin'?" Tham asked.

"I guess I'm all right — I never complain much," the old man said. "I used to complain a lot, but I found it didn't do any good. But I've had a bit of good luck — somebody left another basket at my door last night."

"Well, my goodneth!" Tham said.

"Yes, sir! More grub, and an overcoat, and a shawl for the ole woman."

"That ith thertainly nithe!" Tham told him.

"Sinful waste of money," the old man said. "That overcoat was a good one — last a man ten years easily. And I ain't got more than two or three years longer to live, I reckon. Be a shame for me to spoil that coat."

"Did you thell it?" Tham gasped.

"I sold it to a second-hand thief, and he'd give me only twelve dollars for it. I'll bet it cost three times that — it was brand new. Needed the money much more than I did the coat. Sold the ole woman's shawl, too — her old one is plenty warm enough."

"Well, my goodneth!" Tham exclaimed. "You ought to keep thingth like that when you need 'em."

"Somebody's got a kind heart, or else they're makin' a mistake," the old man said. "I sold the most of the stuff they left last night, but there was some the butcher wouldn't take back. I wish whoever is giving me these things would be careful and leave stuff I can sell back to the store."

"Why, you thilly ath, you ain't thuppothed to thell thingth like that!" Thubway Tham told him. "If you get any more, you thave them for yourthelveth — thee?"

Tham walked on through the alley and went about his business. He was a bit disgusted with the old man, but he told himself that the poor fellow was not quite responsible, since he probably had been half starved for a long time. He'd continue to play Good Samaritan, he would, and maybe he could teach the old man to eat the food left at his door, and to wear the garments provided.

Craddock picked the dip up again that day, much to Thubway Tham's disgust.

"Tham, I would have a few words with you," the detective said.

"Well, thir?"

"Tham, a certain city official was riding in the subway yesterday during the rush hour. He had a well-filled wallet in his clothes. And when he left the subway, he did not have the wallet."

"Ith that pothible!"

"And I have an idea, Tham, that you could tell me something about that leather."

"I, thir? That ith ridiculouth!"

"I'm going to land you one of these days, Tham, and may Heaven and the court have mercy on you when I do. You're running along nice and smooth, old boy, but one of these days you're going to stub your toe, and then it'll be my turn to laugh. You can't get away with it forever, Tham; nobody can. Do you grasp me?"

"Oh, I grathp you, all right, but I don't know what you mean," Tham said.

"You'll realize what it means when you hear the judge remark that the State will board you for several years, old boy. They've got the cell all cleaned out and a new pair of blankets ready for you. The barber has sharpened his clippers and is ready to give you the regular prison hair cut."

"Yeth?" Tham said.

"Yes!" said Craddock. "That's just a little thought for today."

"Thankth for the thought," Tham said. "And now you let me tell you thomething. Every time thome thilly thimp getth hith wallet nicked in the old thubway, you blame it on me. To hear you tell it, you ath, I am the only man in thith world that could lift a leather in a thubway train. I thuppothe anybody elthe would get paralythith if they tried it! If the clock on the Metropolitan tower lotheth a minute, you think I took it. Thimp!"

"I'm wise to you, Tham, all right."

"If you are withe, I am King Tholomon himself, ath I told you onthe before. If you are withe, I am a college profethor with a thring of initialth after my name. You make me thick!"

"Just the same, old boy, I'm going to pay a little more attention to you after this," Craddock told him.

Tham knew that the detective meant it, too. Tham guessed that the detective's superior officer had been making sarcastic remarks about the robberies in the subway. Craddock was no fool, he was a foe to watch — and Thubway Tham knew it. But Tham always had liked such a battle of wits.

"Are you contemplating a ride in our beautiful subway today?" asked Craddock.

"Not if you are," Tham told him. "The thubway ith no plathe when the air ith bad!"

"Meaning I'm rotten, I suppose."

"Ath a man in general, you are all to the muthtard," Tham said, "but ath a detective you are jutht decayed matter."

"Yes?"

"Yeth!" said Thubway Tham.

He turned up the street, knowing well that Craddock was following at his heels. But he did not make an attempt to enter the subway. Tham had a hunch that it would be better not to attempt to work this noon rush hour, and Tham always played the hunches he received.

Much to the surprise of Detective Craddock, Tham went into a motion picture show and sat through a film that had to do with the adventures of an impossible sort of man who could do anything or any-body. Craddock hated picture shows, but he watched Tham while Tham watched the film.

And then Tham went down the street a few blocks and entered another movie palace, much to the disgust of Craddock. This place was jammed, and Tham fought his way to the center of a row, so that Craddock had to remain in another row and at some distance from him.

Craddock watched here for a dodge but it appeared that Thubway Tham was enjoying the comedy that was being flashed upon the screen — which he was. The end of the show came, and immediately there was a jam of persons trying to get out, and another jam trying to get in — for this was a cheap theater that let its patrons fight for seats and did not believe in paying out good money for ushers.

Craddock grunted a curse and made for the doorway. He realized now what Thubway Tham had planned — a get away in the crowd. He watched the front entrance, and he tried to overlook the little exit at the side, but he did not see Thubway Tham.

"Gave me the slip!" Craddock said mournfully. "I'll get that little rat yet — and I'll get him good!"

OUT OF the theater and free of Craddock, Thubway Tham rushed for the nearest subway entrance and plunged into it. He caught an uptown train and looked around for a victim. Fate was kind to him. He left the train a couple of stations further on, and he carried with him a purse that did not belong to him.

The purse netted Tham only fifteen dollars, but he did not attempt to get another. Some sixth sense seemed to warn him that it would be disastrous to do so today. He got rid of the purse and put the three five-dollar bills in his vest pocket, and made his way to the lower end of town again.

Detective Craddock picked him up — and this time he shadowed from a distance. Craddock wanted to catch Thubway Tham off guard. That was the way to land him, Craddock had decided. Craddock was noted as a "shadow," too. He had been using the wrong methods, he declared to himself. He would hang on to Thubway Tham like a flea to a dog and wait patiently for the moment when Thubway Tham would stub his toe.

THAM WAS blissfully ignorant of all this, and he would not have cared had he known. He purchased another basket late in the evening and had it filled with provisions, bought another shawl for the old man's wife, and put the remainder of the fifteen dollars in an envelope and tucked the envelope into one end of the basket.

CROUCHED IN the alley, Detective Craddock watched the light in the room that, he knew, Thubway Tham had for his own. He watched the two exits of the old lodging house, too. He saw the light go out, and he saw Tham emerge from the building with a heavy basket on his arm.

Craddock admitted to himself that he was puzzled. He had seen Tham buy the provisions and fill the basket, and that mystified him. And then he had a sudden thought.

Perhaps Thubway Tham was caring for some criminal who was "hiding out." Perhaps he was carrying provisions to some murderer or burglar badly wanted by the police. Craddock made up his mind to follow and watch. Possibly he would make a capture and at the same time nab Thubway Tham for aiding a fugitive from justice.

Tham slipped down the dark alley, and Detective Craddock followed him noiselessly. Tham put the basket before the door, knocked, and ran. Without making the slightest noise, Detective Craddock ran after him.

Craddock watched while Tham stopped against a wall and looked back at the shack. He saw the old man open the door and pick up the basket. And then, as Thubway Tham started back toward the lodging house, Craddock reached out and nabbed him.

"What's the big idea?" he wanted to know.

"Thir?" Tham gasped. Tham was greatly surprised.

"I've been watching you for hours," Craddock told him. "I saw you buy that basket and that grub. I saw you put it by the door, knock and run. What's the idea?"

"Well, my goodneth!" Thubway Tham cried out. "You make me thick, Craddock! Ith it not pothible for a man to do a kind deed in thith thity without you tryin' to thtop him?"

"I don't quite get this," Craddock said.

"I never knew a thing about it until a couple of dayth ago," Tham told him. "You know how long I have lived in thith alley? Well, I never thaw that thack until then. Craddock, an old man and hith wife live there like dogth. I never thaw thuch mithery. He hath had bad luck for yearth, he told me. No money, no friendth — nothin'. He hath a little hand-organ that maketh a noithe like a bad dream, and he trieth to play it and make hith livin'. It ith awful, Craddock."

"You've been doing a little charity work, is that it?" Detective Craddock asked.

"Yeth, thir!"

"Kind heart, eh?"

"I ain't got much, but I thought I would give them poor folkth thomething to eat," Tham said.

Detective Craddock threw back his head and allowed a volume of raucous laughter to roll from his throat. He leaned against the wall of a building and held his sides and laughed until the tears ran down his fat cheeks.

"What ith the joke, you thimp?" Thubway Tham demanded angrily. "It ith thomething to laugh at, I thuppothe — an old man and hith wife almoth thtarvin' to death!"

"W-wait a minute, Tham!" Craddock gasped. "You don't know these people, I suppose?"

"No, thir. I didn't even athk the old man hith name. It ith none of my buthineth. But he ith thtarvin', and I jutht wanted to help —"

Craddock's gale of laughter interrupted him again.

"You ought to get acquainted with your neighbors, Tham," he said. "I thought everybody knew that old man. He's a licensed street musician in theory, but licensed beggar in practice, and he's a good one. The way he rakes in the nickels and dimes is a caution. And that it not all, Tham. He owns about fifteen houses that he rents."

"What ith that?"

"He is Miser Dan, you fool — known to half the people in town. He lives this way because he hates to spend a cent; begs scraps of food and begs for old clothes. His wife is just as bad. They own a nice string of rental properties in a good part of the city, I happen to know, since I rent my house from the old skinflint. He gathers the rents himself and always tries to beg something on the side. It's a year's job to get him to make repairs. Why, Tham, you ass, the old miser is worth almost fifty thousand dollars! And he was arrested last year for trying to dodge his income tax!"

Thubway Tham leaned weakly against the building. Detective Craddock laughed on.

"What a thimp I am!" Tham muttered.

He walked slowly up the alley and entered the lodging house. Detective Craddock let him go.

IV.

THE THIRST for vengeance was born in the soul of Thubway Tham that night. So he had been purloining purses and running the chances of a long term in prison to give food to a rich miser, had he? And that rich miser had even sold back to the stores the food Tham had purchased. Tham knew, too, that Craddock would tell the story all over town. He'd pass it to other officers who knew Thubway Tham, and he'd drop in here and there and relate it to persons connected with the underworld. Everywhere Thubway Tham went for a time, he would hear about how he fed the miser!

He discovered this the following day. Craddock picked him up and grinned.

"Give Miser Dan his breakfast?" Craddock asked.

Tham glared at him and walked on up the street. He met a few acquaintances, and he knew from their words and manners that they were aware of what had happened. He knew that Craddock had told the story already, and he began to hate Craddock more.

But it was Miser Dan upon whom Tham's desire for vengeance was centered. Tham made his way through the alley, trying to keep the rage from showing in his face, and found the old man sitting before the door of the shack.

"How do you feel thith mornin'?" Tham asked as usual.

"Only tolerable," said Miser Dan. "Some kind friend left me another basket last night. I wish they'd leave salt pork and such instead of this other stuff — I never did like rich food. Seems a sort of waste to me."

"No doubt," Tham said darkly.

"I took the canned goods back to the store and sold them, and I sold the basket. The ole woman took a fancy to the last shawl, and I had to let her have it. Sinful waste. But you've got to humor a woman now and then. She doesn't need that shawl a bit more than you do."

"When do you go out with that hand-organ of yourth?" Tham asked.

"I'm not going out today. I've got to go way uptown to see a man. He said something about getting me a job. It's a long walk, and I'd better be starting, I guess. I'd like to ride on the subway, but that takes money."

"I'll buy you a ticket," Tham said.

"Oh, that'd be too much trouble, sir," said Miser Dan. "If you will just give me the nickel, that will be enough — and thank you."

"I'll buy the ticket!" Tham repeated. "I didn't say I'd give you a nickel — I said I'd give you a ride on the subway."

Miser Dan hobbled up the street behind him. Thubway Tham bought him the ticket and started him toward the gate, and then skipped back up the stairs to the street. He stood on the corner and began to plan. And then he saw and heard something that almost caused him to commit murder. Miser Dan had emerged from the subway and was trying to sell the ticket to a messenger boy for four cents!

Thubway Tham saw red for a moment. Miser Dan started up the street, walking rapidly for one of his age, and Tham started to shadow him as well as detective ever had shadowed Thubway Tham himself.

Block after block the old man went. He got out of the congested business district, followed a cross street, and finally came to a section of small houses set close together.

Thubway Tham watched him from a distance. Tham was almost exhausted because of the long walk. But he was satisfied now, for he realized the truth — Miser Dan was collecting his rents.

The old man had no thought save for money, and he did not notice that Thubway Tham watched him from a distance. He made the rounds of his houses and started back down the street. He came to a tiny park and there sat down on a bench for a time to rest.

Tham crept as close to him as possible and hid behind a clump of brush to watch. Miser Dan had an old wallet, and he was counting bills and putting them into it. When he had finished, he tied the wallet with a piece of twine — and put it into his hip pocket.

"The old thkinflint!" Thubway Tham told himself. "He hath no more thenthe than that. He ith a crook! He leadth a man to believe that he ith thtarvin', and he ith rich. He ith ath crooked ath — ath —"

Miser Dan patted the pocket that contained the wallet, arose from the park bench, buttoned his ragged coat, and started down the street. Thubway Tham followed at a distance; he did not dare approach too closely here, for Miser Dan might turn around and recognize him, and that would interfere with Thubway Tham's plans.

Block after block they walked, until they came to the congested district again. Tham hoped that Miser Dan would take the subway, but he did not. The miser did not care to waste a nickel. He might wear out shoe leather, but he got his old shoes by begging anyway.

Now Thubway Tham edged nearer and awaited a proper opportunity. As a usual thing, Tham never picked a pocket except in a subway train, but this was not a usual occasion. Thubway Tham was not after profit particularly — he was after vengeance.

He knew that the worst thing he could do to Miser Dan would be to get the wallet that contained the rent money. That would be worse than torture or sudden death to the old miser. He would grieve over it for months to come, bewail his fate — and he would get little sympathy from anybody.

"The thimp!" Tham mused. "He ith ath crooked ath —"

There was a crowd on a corner, and Tham quickened his pace, hoping to accomplish his object as Miser Dan went through the crowd. But the old man happened to take it into his mind at that juncture to cross the street, and Tham did not dare make the attempt.

On they went, block after block. They passed Madison Square and they passed Union Square and they went below Washington Square. Thubway Tham wiped the perspiration from his forehead and told himself that he could not endure another mile of it, and that he did not understand how Miser Dan stood it at all.

Now they were in a section of narrow streets and masses of hurrying, jostling humanity. Miser Dan entered a butcher shop and tried to beg some scraps of meat. Thubway Tham waited, grateful for the chance to rest. Dan came forth without the meat, the butcher having recognized him, and started on down the street. Tham knew that he would have to do his work soon now, if he did it at all. And then he saw Detective Craddock.

Craddock was approaching him from the other direction. Thubway Tham did not care to be seen. If he was, Craddock would hold him in conversation for a time, and he would lose Miser Dan. And if Craddock saw Miser Dan, and Tham close behind him, and Dan complained later about being robbed —

Tham darted into a doorway and almost held his breath as Craddock went past. He waited a time, and then went forth into the street again and hurried after the miser. It took him three blocks to catch up.

"Ath crooked ath —" Tham began.

Ahead of him there was a sudden turmoil. A small riot had started from an argument between strikers and strike breakers before a small manufacturing institution. Thubway Tham ran forward now, for he knew that this was his chance. He got within a few feet of Miser Dan, who was being jostled this way and that by the rush of men, and who was trying to get away.

The old man staggered back as somebody gave him an elbow in his ribs. He raised his hands to ward off a second blow — and Thubway Tham did his work.

Darting out from the crowd Tham hurried for the nearest alley. He untied the old wallet, extracted the bills, and hurled the wallet behind a pile of brick. He came to the next street and turned into it, safe, rejoicing.

"The old thkinflint!" Tham said. "Maketh a man think that he ith thtarvin' when he ith rich! He ith ath crooked ath —"

He stopped in a sheltered doorway to investigate his loot. The currency amounted to more than one hundred dollars.

"Thith will make him mourn for a month," Tham murmured. "Let it be a lethon to the thcoundrel! Mither Dan, ith he? He ith ath crooked ath — ath crooked ath Pearl Street!"

THUBWAY THAM'S CHRITHTMATH

THERE was a flurry of fine snow in the stinging air as Thubway Tham came to a stop at a corner of Madison Square, the collar of his overcoat turned up and his gloved hands thrust deep down into the pockets.

It was a little after seven o'clock on Christmas Eve, and Thubway Tham had been purchasing presents. He had them in his pockets now — a new pipe for "Nosey" Moore, who conducted the lodging house where Tham had a room he called home, and a duplicate of it for Detective Craddock.

Thubway Tham chuckled at the thought of a pickpocket of the professional variety giving a Christmas present to the detective assigned to watch him and capture him if he could. But the relationship between himself and Detective Craddock was peculiar in many ways. Each considered the other a foe-man worthy of his steel. For almost two years Detective Craddock had been trying to catch Thubway Tham "with the goods," that being the only way in which he could land the little dip in the big gray prison up the river, but the detective's efforts had availed him nothing.

And now Thubway Tham stood back against a building and watched the happy, jostling crowd. Men rushed here and there, their arms filled with bundles of odd shapes and sizes. Women chatted gayly as they hurried toward the nearest subway entrances. The people seemed happy, and the weather was just right. Tham felt that it was going to be a good Christmas.

He watched the throng for a time, and then lighted a cigarette, took half a dozen puffs at it to get it going properly, bent his head against the force of the stinging wind, and crossed the street to enter Madison Square.

Though it was far too cold to sit on a bench, Thubway Tham wandered from force of habit to the corner where he did sit on pleasant afternoons. He was hoping that he might run across Detective Craddock — and he did.

Just then the big officer came slowly along the walk, chewing at a cigar and watching those who passed. As they met, Craddock grinned.

"Tho I thee your ugly fathe again, do I?" Thubway Tham said by way of greeting.

"Even so, Tham! This is indeed an unexpected pleasure," Detective Craddock told him. "I little expected to run across you in this part of our fair city at this hour of the evening. I had a lurking suspicion that you traveled toward the south when dusk came and remained in that section about which the least said the better."

"Ith that tho?" Tham wanted to know. "And what ith the matter with the part of town in which I live?"

"There is nothing the matter with that part of town, Tham, but some of the people there are under suspicion."

"Uh-huh! Everybody ith under thuthpithion if we leave it to thome of you withe copperth," Tham said. "I wath jutht thtandin' here watchin' the crowd."

"It'll bear watching — in spots," Detective Craddock retorted, grinning again.

"Tho?"

"So! It certainly gratifies me, Tham, to find you out in the open like this. Were you in the subway, now, I'd have to keep an eye on you continually, and I have other things to do this evening. Men of your ilk, Tham, are especially active in the happy Christmas throngs."

"Ith that tho? My goodneth!" Thubway Tham gasped out. "Any crook who would thteal from a perthon on Chrithtmath Eve ought to be thot at thunrithe."

"Tham, that sentiment, coming from you, rather surprises me," the detective admitted.

"You thay, Craddock, that I am a dip and —"

"I'll say again that you are!"

"Maybe tho! But, if I do happen to be a dip — and I ain't thayin' that I am — take it from me that I would not work on a night like thith!"

"No?"

"No!" Thubway Tham declared earnestly. "There are dayth and dayth on which a dip can work. And if one thtealth from a man or woman what might be money for Chrithtmath prethentth, it would be bad luck."

"Oh, I see! I'm getting a new angle on crook superstition!" Craddock said.

"It ith not thuperthtition — it ith jutht common dethenthy!" Thubway Tham declared. "I would go hungry before I would thteal on Chrithtmath Eve!"

"And I believe that you actually mean it!" Detective Craddock exclaimed. "I feel greatly relieved, Tham. I won't have to shadow you tonight."

"You couldn't thadow an elephant," Tham told him. "Craddock, you are a copper, but you're dethent and have thome thenthe. I'll thay that much."

"Thank you kindly!" said Craddock, bowing.

"And tho," Thubway Tham added, pulling a little package from one of his big overcoat pockets, "I have gone and bought you a Chrithtmath prethent."

"Tham, you overwhelm me!" the detective declared. "This is not offered in — er — in the nature of a bribe?"

"Craddock, don't be an ath!"

"I humbly beg your pardon, Tham. Thanks! A pipe!"

"You thmoke, don't you?"

"I do, and I happen to need a new pipe. I'll have a little present for you tomorrow, Tham, if I happen to run across you. But understand me, old-timer, I'd take you in this minute if I had the goods on you."

"That ith underthtood," Tham replied. "When you get the goodth on me, Craddock, I'd ought to be taken in and given twithe the limit. I'll thay I had!"

"Nevertheless, old boy, one of these days —"

"I know that old thpeech!" Thubway Tham interrupted. "One of thethe dayth you are goin' to catch me dead to rightth and thend me up the river for about fifteen or twenty yearth. Uh-huh! It theemth to me that I have been hearin' that thtory for quite thome little time now. But

I'll thay thith much, Craddock — if I ever am taken in, I hope you'll be the copper to do it and get all the credit."

"Thank you kindly, again!"

"Even if you are a thort of thimp at timeth," Tham added. "Merry Chrithtmath!"

Detective Craddock grinned as Thubway Tham continued along the walk, looked at the pipe and put it into his pocket, and then walked briskly in the opposite direction, toward a corner where he believed that he had important business. Some pickpocket, it had been reported, was working there.

Thubway Tham meant what he had said. He never lifted a leather on Christmas Eve, or on the Fourth of July. He felt sure that it would prove to be ill luck. Of course, if there were extenuating circumstances, he might feel called upon to do so — but he never had met such extenuating circumstances.

He crossed over to Broadway and walked slowly in the direction of Times Square. There, he had decided, he would take a subway express for downtown, go to the lodging house of Nosey Moore, give Mr. Moore his pipe, and then retire.

Though he had few real friends in the world, Thubway Tham felt happy. The spirit of Christmas was upon him. It was as though the folks of the world were all in one big family, and he belonged. He purchased newspapers he did not want and gave them back to the newsboys. He bought a sprig of holly and put it in the buttonhole of his lapel. When men and women jostled him and almost knocked him off the walk and into the street, Thubway Tham did not glare, as he would have glared on any other day.

Descending into the subway, Thubway Tham waited on the crowded platform until a downtown express roared in and boarded one of the crowded cars. As the train started its dash through the big tube, Tham could not help wishing that it was not Christmas Eve. Here were so many "business" chances!

Tham saw half a dozen men near him, any one of whom would have been a prospective victim had he been at "work." But he did not contemplate breaking his rule. There were no extenuating circumstances, as far as he could see.

He glanced around at the happy faces, listened to meaningless chatter, yawned once or twice. He pulled off his gloves and dropped them into an overcoat pocket. It was hot in the crowded car.

And then his eyes bulged suddenly!

Within six feet of him he saw a small-sized man deliberately "lift a leather."

Thubway Tham experienced mingled emotions. In the first place it was unpardonable to lift a leather on Christmas Eve, and the man who did it deserved bad luck for a year. In the next place the subway was sacred to Thubway Tham. All recognized crooks realized that fact and left the subway strictly to Tham. And here was some man Tham did not know lifting a leather on a forbidden day, and doing it in the subway.

"Why, the dirty thneak!" Thubway Tham growled to himself. "It would therve him right if —"

A sudden idea came to Tham. He glanced at the pickpocket and then at the man standing to the right of the pickpocket. Yes, that was the victim, Tham felt sure; the man's overcoat was dark gray, and it was through the flap of a dark gray overcoat that the pickpocket had reached to lift the wearer's wallet. Well, the crook had nerve to continue to stand beside his victim.

"I'll bet that poor fellow needth the money," Tham told himself. "Maybe it ith Chrithtmath money! And that dirty thneak touched him for hith purthe right before my eyeth. Hith work wath coarthe at that!"

Tham's idea was completed by this time. He would touch the dip in turn, he decided, and restore the purse to its owner. That would be a kind act, and Christmas was the time for kind acts, the way Tham saw things.

He swayed forward as the train dashed around a curve and got nearer the pickpocket. He awaited his chance, when the train was coming into the station. His hand darted forward, the purse was taken, and slipped down into Tham's overcoat pocket.

The train stopped, the doors went open, and the owner of the purse got out. Tham stepped out of the car behind him and tried to catch him before he got up to the street. He managed it as the street was reached and touched the other man on the arm.

"Well?" the other said snappily as he turned.

Tham had not expected such a surly tone, but he told himself that perhaps this man had troubles. He grinned and extended the pocket-book.

"You dropped your purthe, thir," Thubway Tham said. "Here it ith!"

The other man looked at him blankly for an instant.

"My — oh, yes, my purse!" he exclaimed. "And you picked it up, I suppose?"

"Thomething like that," Tham admitted.

"Um! And how does it happen that you didn't keep it?" the other asked snapping the purse open.

"That would be a dirty trick on Chrithtmath Eve," Thubway Tham told him. "That ith right — open it and count the money. Think that I thtole thome of it?"

"Certainly not, my man," the other responded. "Had you been wanting to steal, I suppose you would have retained the whole thing. Let me see! A hundred and five — that is correct! Here!"

He extended a five-dollar bill toward Thubway Tham.

"I wath not thinkin' of getting any reward for returnin' the purthe," Tham said.

"Yes, I appreciate that fact, my man, but you are going to take this five just the same," the other replied. "Buy yourself something for Christmas — anything you like. And — thanks! I thank you very much! I — er — appreciate this!"

Thubway Tham accepted the bill. "That ith all right, thir," he said.

And then the other man smiled and turned away. Thubway Tham looked after him and grinned. It struck Tham as funny that he should return a purse stolen by somebody else, and one that still held a hundred dollars, and get a reward for doing it.

Tham was several blocks from the establishment of Nosey Moore, but it was not so cold now, and Thubway Tham decided that he would walk the remainder of the distance rather than descend into the subway again and wait for a train. So he went off down the busy street less than half a block behind the man to whom he had returned the stolen purse.

He had lifted a leather on Christmas Eve, but there had been extenuating circumstances, Tham told himself. He had stolen from a thief and returned the loot to its owner. Tham felt a sudden glow that came from what he considered a kind deed well done. He promised himself that he would spend that five dollars for something that he could keep as a memento of the occasion.

Three blocks down the street he went, and then he came to a sudden stop where some children were singing in the street. Tham waited at the edge of the crowd, already feeling in a pocket for a coin to give when the collection was gathered. He heard two men talking to one side, and when he turned, thinking that he recognized one of the voices, he saw that it was the man to whom he had returned the purse.

"I call it rich!" the man was saying. "The fellow made a mistake, naturally. He saw somebody drop a purse and ran after me and handed it back, thinking that it was mine. A hundred and five in it, too. I gave the boob a five for his honesty, and he broke his tongue thanking me!"

At that his companion laughed.

"Ha, ha!" laughed the man to whom Tham had returned the purse. "A cool hundred to the good! Here it is — see? I'll put it with this other hundred of mine, roll it all together. Some little celebration we'll have tomorrow!" At that he discarded the leather, and a few moments later Thubway Tham picked it up, opened it and found that it contained a card bearing the owner's name and address; then tucked it safely away in an inside pocket.

Thubway Tham felt his blood boiling. So! He had believed that he was doing a kind act, and this man — this crook — had taken advantage of it! And now he was boasting, and calling Thubway Tham a boob! That was the worst of it!

It seemed to Tham that he saw red for a moment. He wanted an instant revenge! He wanted to get back that money, since it did not belong to the man to whom he had given it.

Here, Tham told himself, were extenuating circumstances. If he committed a robbery on this man it would be a just affair. But here was no leather to lift. The scoundrel had wrapped the bills around his own hundred dollars and had put the roll into his coat pocket. Getting it would be more difficult than lifting a leather after the established fashion.

Yet Tham was determined. He forgot all thought of Christmas. He forgot superstition and the season and remembered only that he must get that roll of bills.

When the two men started down the street, Thubway Tham followed them through the crowd. He did not even see the little girl who held out a hat for a coin now that the singing was at an end. He saw nothing except the scoundrel who had duped him.

And Tham felt ill at ease, too, because this was not in the subway, where he generally worked. He did not want to make the attempt until he was reasonably sure of success. Thubway Tham did not wish to spend Christmas Day in prison, waiting for trial on a serious charge. And the true story, if told, would not be believed and would not help him if it was believed.

He remained just far enough behind to avoid being seen and recognized by the man to whom he had given the purse. On down the street they went through the joyous, jostling throng. They approached another corner where young street singers were at work, and Tham thought that possibly he might make the attempt there, if his prospective victim stopped to listen to the singing.

They stopped. Thubway Tham glanced around quickly, searching for the best getaway in case ill luck befell him. He glanced back — and was in time to witness a scene.

Detective Craddock was plowing his way through the crowd. Tham thought at first that the detective was coming straight to him to engage him in conversation and spoil his chances for getting the money back. Craddock had journeyed downtown on police business, he supposed, and it was bad fortune that he should appear at this corner at this particular time.

But Craddock, it was evident, had not seen Thubway Tham. He went around the edge of the crowd. Three quick steps forward the detective took — and touched on the shoulder the man to whom Thubway Tham had given the purse!

"I want you, Canderon!" Craddock said.

There was a curse and a short scuffle. Tham shuddered.

"Now, take it easy!" he heard Detective Craddock saying. "We've been looking for you for five or six months. You were foolish to come back to town so soon, Canderon. We'll take a little trip to headquarters now. As for your friend —"

But Canderon's companion had darted into the crowd and disappeared.

"Probably somebody else that's wanted badly," Craddock said. "Come along, Canderon!"

The detective scattered the immediate crowd with a few growls and led his prisoner away. Thubway Tham slipped after them. Confound it! Craddock had spoiled things now! What fate was it that had brought Craddock there just at the wrong minute? Was Thubway Tham to lose his chance for revenge?

Craddock, he knew, was bound for a patrol box on the next corner, there to flash a message for the wagon. There seemed little chance for Thubway Tham to do anything.

Tham remembered that roll of bills in the man's pocket. He wanted the roll. He wanted the hundred dollars, and he wanted Conderon's hundred also, by way of profit and revenge. And the presence of Craddock spoiled things!

"Yeth, the thimp!" Tham said growlingly to himself. "Why couldn't he have found hith man a few minuteth later? Thith ith what I get for givin' him a Chrithtmath prethent!"

Detective Craddock went directly to the patrol box, paying no attention to the low mouthings of the prisoner. Tham followed a few feet behind. Curious ones stopped to turn and stare. They came to the patrol box, and Craddock sent in his call and waited.

Thubway Tham was desperate now. His chance to get that roll of bills was lost, he told himself. Craddock, even as he thought this, turned and saw him and grinned.

"Why, hello, Tham," he said.

"Hello, yourthelf!" Tham replied, stepping nearer, "Made a catch, did you?"

"I certainly have, Tham. Mr. Canderon, here, is badly wanted for swindling women and children. Better take a lesson from this, Tham, and lead a straight and honest life. If you don't, I'll be taking you in like this one of these days."

"Yeth?" Tham said. "Maybe tho and maybe not. Tho thith bird hath been swindlin' women, hath he? He lookth like that thort of a cuth. I hope he getth twenty yearth!"

"Tham, wishing bad luck to a brother in crime?"

"He ith no brother of crime of mine," Tham declared stoutly. "I don't care if you hang him!"

"Yes, he'll get a few years to think it over," Craddock replied, chuckling. "He'll eat his Christmas dinner in jail, Tham. You be careful that you don't."

The prisoner had regarded Thubway Tham with amazement at first, and now he turned his face away from the curious throng and looked down the street. Tham stepped a little closer.

"Craddock, lay off that thtuff!" he said in low tones. "Callin' me a crook in front of all thethe folkth? Wonder you wouldn't make them go on about their buthineth!"

Detective Craddock turned quickly to see that the crowd was growing denser and pressing closer. A patrolman came charging through it.

"Need any help, Craddock?" he asked.

"Just send these people about their business," Craddock said.

The patrolman whirled toward the crowd and brandished an arm, meaning that he expected an instant dispersal of the mob. Craddock watched him at the work.

But Mr. Canderon at that moment decided that he did not wish to eat his Christmas dinner in jail if it could be avoided. While Craddock's back was turned, Canderon gave a quick spring forward, knocked Craddock to his knees, and jerked himself free.

Craddock's yell as he struggled to get to his feet caused the patrolman to turn and rush to the rescue. But Thubway Tham had acted already.

Tham saw his chance. He hurled himself forward and thrust out a leg. Mr. Canderon crashed to the pavement, and Tham, with a flying leap, was a-straddle him. There was a sharp, fierce tussle. And then

Craddock and the patrolman were at the scene, a blackjack descended, and Mr. Canderon passed out momentarily.

And then Tham got to his feet and started brushing his clothes. The "wagon" arrived, and the prisoner was turned over. Detective Craddock stepped up to Thubway Tham and slapped him on the shoulder.

"Thanks, Tham!" he said. "Good work! I must be growing careless. But I am rather surprised that you'd help an officer against a crook."

"But there are crookth and crookth," Thubway Tham recited.

"He might have escaped in the crowd. You certainly bowled him over."

"I tripped him," Tham explained.

"A good job, too! Tham, I appreciate it! And that reminds me — I won't be able to see you tomorrow, because when I reported an hour ago I got orders to go to Philadelphia tomorrow and bring back a prisoner. Hot way to spend Christmas."

"Tough luck," Tham commented.

"But you're going to have a Christmas present from me, old-timer! Here is a five-dollar bill. You buy yourself something you really want and tell me about it later."

"Yeth, but —" Tham began.

"Go on and take it, or you'll make me feel mean. And I want to be square with you so, in case I get the chance to land you, I can do it with an easy conscience."

Tham accepted the bill. "Thanks, Craddock!" he said. "Buthineth ith exthellent thith evenin'."

Craddock waved his hand and went down the street. Thubway Tham, chuckling, walked rapidly in the other direction. He had the five Craddock had given him, and the five Canderon had given him for returning the purse — and the two hundred he had lifted from the latter's pocket as they had wrestled across the walk.

Before Thubway Tham went to his room that night he made a little journey to the home of the man whose wallet he was carrying. Tham returned the wallet and with it the one hundred and five dollars it had contained when its owner entered the subway. Joy was in Tham's heart, for he had made glad the heart of another.

"Merry Chrithtmath!" Thubway Tham said with a happy smile as he hurried toward the lodging house of Nosey Moore. "Merry Chrithtmath! I'll thay that it ith!"

THUBWAY THAM'S GLORIOUS FOURTH

"WHEN IN the courthe of human event, it becometh nethethary for one people to ditholve the political bandth which have connected them with another," said Thubway Tham to himself, as he regarded his reflection in the mirror over the wash-stand in his room, "then there ith a holiday born. Tho we have the Gloriouth Fourth!"

Tham crossed the room to the window and looked down at the alley. Before him stretched a vista of rusty tin cans, empty packing cases, tumbledown fences, ramshackle shacks, dirty and ragged children and tired-looking women who labored over washboards. He always had felt a keen interest in the alley dwellers in the district where he lived.

"Even thothe people will thelebrate tomorrow," Thubway Tham told himself. "A man may not have much of thith world'th goodth, and he may cuth the government and hard timeth and think thith world ith a helluva plathe, but he will thelebrate the Gloriouth Fourth. It ith one day when every man in thith country hath a right to yell. Far be it from me to roath other countrieth, but I will thay that the Gloriouth Fourth ith the betht holiday ever thelebrated! I am goin' to thelebrate mythelf!"

Having made that declaration, Thubway Tham turned away from the window and crossed the room again to sit down on the edge of the bed. In police headquarters there was a certain document that told how many inches there were between Tham's eyes, and a lot of other data like that. His photograph was there, and some writing on a corner of a card remarked to those who cared to read that Thubway Tham was a notorious pickpocket, arrested and sentenced to the penitentiary once, and since his release the bane of officers who would like to send him there again.

Being a professional pickpocket did not keep Thubway Tham from being patriotic, however. The man who dresses in a long black coat and makes a speech about the eagle screaming is not always the best patriot. Thubway Tham demonstrated that fact now; for he raised one hand and took a solemn oath that he would not mar the Glorious Fourth by picking a pocket.

"It would be a thin," he told his reflection in the mirror, "to thteal from a man who ith thelebratin' hith country'th birthday. It ith not done in the betht familieth."

It was quite late in the afternoon. Thubway Tham combed his hair, put on his hat, went out upon the street, and walked toward Union Square. He had made a short trip in the subway during the noon rush hour and had obtained possession of a wallet which netted him almost one hundred dollars in currency.

So Tham decided that he would work no more that day — he called it work — partly because he had enough, and partly because he felt a peculiar sort of premonition that seemed to say he would court disaster if he bothered about other people's pockets that evening.

Puffing at a cigarette, he walked up the street slowly, now and then nodding to an acquaintance of the underworld who hurried along in a furtive manner. He stopped at a street-crossing to wait for the stream of traffic to pass — and felt a touch on his arm.

Thubway Tham removed the cigarette from his mouth and turned slowly.

"Tho it ith you!" he said. "I made a bet with mythelf that it wath you, and I win. Are you goin' to pethter me again today?"

Detective Craddock, who had sworn a year or more before to "get" Thubway Tham, grinned down at him.

"Can't a man pass the time of day without rousing your anger?" the detective asked. "Seems to me you're rather touchy lately."

"Tho?"

"Exactly, Thinking of taking a little ride in the subway about the time the trains are crowded with home-going folk?"

"I am not," said Thubway Tham. "The crowdth of home-goin' folkth are nothin' in my young life."

"But their wallets and watches are, eh?"

"I am not thayin' tho!"

"Well, Tham, I've been after you a long time, and I'm willing to admit that you're somewhat smooth. I know you're busy lifting leathers, and I know that I'll have to catch you in the act and have excellent witnesses before I can send you up the river. But I'm going to get you one of these days, boy!"

"You have been thayin' that for thome time now," Thubway Tham reminded him.

"True — too true, Tham. But you'll make a little slip one of these days. You clever birds always do, you know. You can't get away with it forever."

"Perhapth not," Tham told him. "The thity may get withe to itthelf and replathe thome of the men it hath on the polithe forthe with real detectiveth. In that cathe, I'll have to be careful."

Detective Craddock's face flushed, and he fought to keep from losing his temper. He had learned long before that Thubway Tham always made him look ridiculous — and feel that way, too — when he lost his temper.

"Tham," he said, "tomorrow is the Fourth of July. It appears on the surface that it will be celebrated this year with much gusto and considerable noise and merry-making."

"That ith ath it thould be," Tham informed him.

"Which means, naturally, that there will be a few million persons here and hereabouts who will take a frantic notion to celebrate anywhere except in their own houses and flats and rooms, or wherever they eat and sleep. That means, Tham, as no doubt you have guessed some time since, that they will be traveling in throngs. There are some benighted persons who use the surface cars and the elevated, but countless thousands will pay their nickels to the men who operate the subway. The general drift of my few remarks, Tham, is toward the main thought, which is that you undoubtedly will take advantage of the big crowds in the subway trains tomorrow to ply your nefarious trade."

"Thir?"

"You heard me!" said Craddock.

"Yeth, thir,"

"And I'm going to be right at your heels, old boy. We can't have people annoyed on the Glorious Fourth."

"Then why annoy me? Why pethter me?" Thubway Tham demanded. "If I wath a dip, and I am not thayin' that I am, I would not lift a thingle leather on the Fourth."

"Is that the way you feel about it?"

"It ith!"

"Well, Tham, I hate to spend the day following you around. You may be a crook, but you're a man of your word, strange as it may seem. You have a reputation in that respect. Will you give me your word of honor and your sacred promise that you'll pick no pockets this year on the Fourth of July?"

"Thertainly!" Thubway Tham replied instantly. "You have my word of honor."

"Very well, old-timer. We'll call the war off until day after tomorrow, then. May I wish you a happy holiday?"

"You may," said Thubway Tham solemnly.

"How are you going to spend it, if I may ask?"

"Coney Island," replied Tham. "I am goin' to mingle with all the nutth and crazy perthonth. I am goin' to thute the thuteth and bump the humpth, and eat thalt water taffy, and watch the ocean, and all that thilly thtuff."

"Good idea! I may take the wife and kids and do the same thing."

"You jutht thaid that you would not pethter me if I gave you my word, and I did."

"I have no intention, Tham, of pestering you. If by chance I happen to see you at Coney Island, I shall make it a point to look in the opposite direction, unless your actions are suspicious."

Detective Craddock bowed with mock politeness and went on up the street. Thubway Tham removed his cap and scratched his head as he looked after the officer.

"And I thall keep my word!" he promised. "Every wallet in thith man'th town ith thafe from me tomorrow. I can make up for it on the fifth."

II.

THUBWAY THAM arose on the morning of the Glorious Fourth at an hour much earlier than usual, had his breakfast at the little restaurant he frequented, and then made his way to Coney Island.

Though he considered it an early hour, yet he found thousands before him. Heads of families were there, with wives and babies and children of an age to get lost and be found underfoot. The shows and booths were open, and the proprietors thereof ready to make a "killing." Venders of "hot dogs" and popcorn were busy. And the old Atlantic splashed before the scene as if making a dignified attempt to add to the gaiety by taking a part in the celebration.

Having found a place where he could rest and watch the tumbling ocean, Thubway Tham remained there for some time, content to let the breeze blow over him. Bathers already had made their appearance, and Tham exulted in their antics. The day grew older. Somewhere a band blared.

Now Thubway Tham always had had a weakness for brass bands. He got up and walked toward the music, making his way slowly through the crowd, jostling against good-natured men and women, with no thought of lifting a leather. Once the thought came to him that this certainly would be an excellent place in which to ply his trade, but he put the idea away from him. He had promised himself, and he had promised Detective Craddock, and he was a man to keep his word.

Thubway Tham ate popcorn and "hot dogs," went into a picture show, watched the bathers and the dancers, and listened to the music. It was a good thing that the country had a day to celebrate, Thubway Tham thought. He supposed that the great majority did not even stop to remember what they were celebrating, but yet it was good.

Passing down the main street again, once more going toward a dancing pavilion, Thubway Tham found himself caught in a crowd listening to a "spieler" for a side show of some sort. A man may make a promise to himself, Thubway Tham found, but that does not cause him to forget his business training. Tham could not help but notice that a flashily dressed man standing directly in front of him had a well-filled wallet in his hip pocket.

"The thimp!" Tham told himself. "It would therve him right if he lotht that coin!"

He watched the flashily dressed man and did not approve of him.

His clothes were painfully new and his manner brazen. Tham saw him approach a young woman and speak to her, and observed the young woman flush and hurry away.

"The nathty mather!" Tham said.

The man moved ahead, and Thubway Tham followed him. He was certainly an arrogant individual. He appeared to think that any young woman should deem it a privilege to be his companion for the day. The more repulses he received, the more determined became his quest.

They reached the outskirts of the crowd, and there the man in the flashy clothes struck up a conversation with a young woman who seemed willing to talk.

"Be my little playmate, sister," he said. "I've got the price of a good time and nobody to spend it on."

He pulled out the wallet and exhibited a sheaf of bills.

"Been robbing the firm?" the girl asked.

"No need, sister; no need. We have ample funds of our own, let us say. Will you try the 'Rolling Waves' with me?"

"Not this afternoon," the girl answered.

The man grasped her by an arm.

"Won't take that for an answer," he said. "Let's be on our way, sister."

"If I was your sister, I'd teach you a few things," she said.

She broke away from him and hurried through the crowd. Thubway Tham grinned. He of the flashy clothes turned and saw the grin.

"Lost out that time," he announced. "Must have been waiting for her steady, what? Very few girls refuse to help spend a roll."

"Got a roll, have you?" Tham asked without apparent interest.

"I'm rotten with the stuff," the other confided. "Decided I'd have a whale of a time today. Don't seem to be making much progress."

"You'd better not carry that wallet in your hip pocket," Tham told him. "That ith the plathe that ith the delight of all pickpocketh. The firtht thing you know, you'll be minuth thome coin."

"Pickpockets? You cause me merriment," the other said. "Tho?"

"You do. That's an old gag that a man can take a wallet from another man's hip pocket without the owner of the wallet being wise to it. I'd have to be asleep or drunk before a man could hand me a deal like that."

"Think it ith difficult?" Tham asked.

"With me it would be, all right, I'm no more afraid of pickpockets than I am that the Dead Sea will come over here and wash this shore. Pickpockets go after the man who chews a straw, and that's all. They have better sense than try to rob a wise guy."

"Ith that tho? Theemth to me that I heard not very long ago that a thertain withe guy wath touched for hith roll."

"Probably preoccupied," said the other. "Had his mind on his job, or something like that."

Thubway Tham gulped. More than anything else, he wanted to teach this arrogant, all-knowing one a lesson. But he had promised! He felt Temptation tugging at his elbow.

Turning abruptly away, Tham walked toward the water again and leaned against a railing to observe the bathers. In an hour or so he would eat, he decided. He would remain for the fireworks in the evening and go home, tired and happy, with the last crowds.

Temptation, standing beside him, began to point out loot. Within the half hour Thubway Tham saw no less than half a dozen prospective victims. There was a fat man whose wallet showed plainly in a hip pocket. There was a man who stuffed a roll of bills into a waistcoat pocket while Thubway Tham watched him. Another glanced at a watch that was studded with jewels and slipped it back into his pocket carelessly. Thubway Tham knew that it would be child's play for him to get that watch.

He left the beach and journeyed on, almost sorry that he had made a promise to himself and Detective Craddock. And then he met Craddock face to face.

"Well, well!" the detective said. "Having a good time, Tham?"

"Yeth, thir."

"Been behaving yourself?"

"I gave you my promithe."

"I beg your pardon, Tham. I should think it would make you nervous to be around this crowd. There are so many careless persons in it."

"And that ith the truth."

"Been observing some of them, have you?"

"Ath if a man could help it!" Thubway Tham declared. "But a promithe ith a promithe. You havin' a good time?"

"On special duty," Craddock replied. "Couldn't even bring the wife and kiddies along. Watching for dips."

"Yeth?"

"Yes. And there have been some at work, too; take it from me. Complaints have been coming in by the score."

"If you think that I —"

"I don't!" Craddock interrupted, "If this was the subway, now, I might think differently."

"You are goin' to keep talkin' until you thpoil my Gloriouth Fourth thelebration," Tham complained. "Ain't you got any thenthe? Want to talk thop all the time?"

"I humbly beg your pardon, Tham, and will hie me on my way," Detective Craddock returned.

He was as good as his promise, and Temptation, having been lurking in the background while Tham talked to Craddock, came forward again and once more touched Tham's elbow.

Thubway Tham beheld in front of him an obese gentleman who radiated prosperity. He seemed to be in charge of two young women who called him uncle. Tham thought it was a very pleasant family party at first, until he heard the obese gentleman talk.

"Go as far as you like!" he told his nieces. "Uncle cleaned up a nice little pile last week. Uncle caught 'em when they were going down, and bought and held 'em until they went up, thereby stinging a few financial enemies. Uncle has the goods. Go as far as you like in this simple-minded merry-making."

Tham chuckled to himself. Uncle continued his conversation, and the tune of it was business and yet more business, and money-making, and gouging financial opponents. Tham began to feel a sort of rage, especially when one of the pretty nieces asked her uncle to drop his business talk, at least for the remainder of the Fourth.

"The thimp ith long on coin and thort on brainth," Tham mused.

"He ith the kind of man I like to touch for hith roll. If thith wath not the Gloriouth Fourth —"

Thubway Tham turned away, but Temptation remained at his heels.

Before the end of another hour the perspiration was standing out on Tham's forehead. Never before, in a single day, had Thubway Tham seen so many opportunities for success in his own particular line. It grew to be an agony to him.

He returned to the pavilion and watched the maze of dancers, wishing for the moment that he was younger, and not a crook, and had a pretty girl, and could dance. Tham began feeling lonely. He wished that he had somebody to help him celebrate. He had not asked any of his underworld friends to accompany him, fearing they would laugh at him.

Out in the crowd again, he found himself attracted to a boy about eight years of age. The youngster grinned at him and announced that he was lost. Tham adopted him.

"We will jutht drift along with the crowd, and maybe you will thee your folkth," Thubway Tham said. "And, meanwhile, you will be my guetht. Thee?"

The idea tickled Thubway Tham. He prowled through the crowd, holding the youngster by one hand. He bought the boy ice cream and soda and popcorn, took him for a ride on the merry-go-round, and treated him to any amusement he showed an interest in.

Craddock came across him again.

"What's the big idea? Turning family man?" the detective asked.

"Thith boy ith lotht, and we are tryin' to find hith folkth," Tham explained. "And I am fillin' him up on popcorn and peanutth."

Craddock slapped Tham on the back. He had three youngsters at home.

"Good boy!" he exclaimed. "Tham, you're too good to be a dip. Why don't you get a decent job and quit the crook game?"

"Ith that any way to talk?" Tham demanded, glancing down at the boy. "On your way, Craddock. You are the biggetht petht in thith man'th town!"

Ten minutes later a semi-hysterical woman descended upon Thubway Tham and the boy, grasped the latter in her arms, and glared at the former.

"He wath lotht and I found him," Tham explained. "We have been thelebratin' the Gloriouth Fourth. Maybe I fed him too much ithe cream, I dunno. But it hath been a pleathure."

He hurried away before the woman could pour forth her thanks. He went down to the beach again and sat down.

"Craddock ith an ath!" he declared. "I tried to be thraight onthe, and everybody bunkoed me. But I with I did have a boy like that, jutht to buy popcorn for."

Thubway Tham propped himself comfortably against a box that happened to be near, pulled his hat down over his eyes, and gave himself up to thought. It was growing dark now, and Coney Island had flashed forth in all its splendor. Thubway Tham felt lonesome. He wished for bosom friends. He had done his best to enjoy a day of celebration and had been on his good behavior, and he felt that it had netted him little.

"I'll be moanin' in a minute," he told himself. "There thould not be holidayth for a man like me."

The darkness came, and the fireworks began. Thubway Tham forgot his momentary lonesomeness and enjoyed the spectacle. He listened to the band again, and watched the dancers, and saw the families starting for their homes, tired but happy, the children who remained awake talking of the wonders of the day. There seemed to be half a million babies sleeping in mothers' arms.

Tham had eaten dinner and had partaken of refreshments until he wished for no more. There seemed to be nothing left to do except go home. At that hour of the night Coney Island was no place for a man without a friend.

So Thubway Tham decided to return to Manhattan and seek his bed. He half wished that he had not promised himself and Craddock to be on his good behavior. It might liven things up if he could "lift a leather."

III.

ON HIS way to the city Thubway Tham slumbered a bit. He was thinking deeply of unusual things. He had obtained a seat, and the aisle was jammed with humanity. Now and then this mass of persons surged this way and that as some got off or more got on.

Thubway Tham heard a well-remembered voice, came to himself, and looked up. He of the flashy clothes was standing in the aisle, trying to make the acquaintance of two girls.

"The ath!" Tham muttered.

He heard another voice, and saw the uncle and the two nieces. Temptation was present again to Thubway Tham.

At Brooklyn Bridge Tham left the elevated train with the crowd and walked down to the subway entrance. He was chagrined to find that the two men did the same. Tham felt his anger growing. Was it not possible for a man to be honest for a day? Were wallets to be flaunted continually in the face of a professional pickpocket on a day when he had sworn to keep his hands to himself?

Tham boarded an uptown subway train, and so did the other men. The grip of Temptation was tightening on Thubway Tham. Something seemed to tell him that he should take the wallet of the flashily dressed man who had boasted that such a thing could not be done, and of the obese individual who talked of business and money while on a holiday with two pretty nieces.

"A pair of atheth!" Tham said, and moved closer to them.

Habit, environment, his own skill, all affected him. He inspected the persons in the car and could see no officer of the law he knew. He fought to resist Temptation, but felt himself growing weaker.

Thubway Tham passed the station where he should have left the car. It seemed that he could not take his eyes off the two men, who stood not far apart. Something seemed to be pulling him toward them. Nervously wetting his lips Thubway Tham glanced around again. Craddock was almost at his elbow. "Great day, eh?" the detective asked.

"Thome thelebration!" Tham admitted, glad for once that Craddock was at hand. "And thome tired crowd!"

"I'm tired myself," Craddock admitted. "I'll get a day off tomorrow for this."

"Yeth?"

"Yes. You've been taking a day off today, I understand."

Craddock eyed him narrowly.

"Thertainly!" said Tham. "I thaid I would do it, and I did."

"I'm never quite sure about you, Tham."

Thubway Tham felt enraged. After all the fat wallets he had passed by, to have Detective Craddock talk like that! His face flushed, and he gasped.

"Nobody but a thimp of a detective," he said, "would doubt the word of a gentleman."

"So?"

"Tho! You make me thick, Craddock! There ith a head of cabbage where your brainth thould be."

"Yes?"

"Yeth! If you are a thample of what ith on the polithe forthe, no wonder there are tho many crookth in thith man'th town! You are an invitation to every crook in the world!"

"Don't let it worry you, Tham," Craddock said. "And don't get so touchy just because I intimated that you might have broken your word. Words have been broken before now. And you're riding pretty far uptown, aren't you?"

"I am," said Thubway Tham. "But I am goin' to get off at Twenty-third Threet and walk back. The air ith nithe and cool."

Craddock turned to speak to another acquaintance, and Thubway Tham glared at the back of his head. His day had been spoiled. He had promised to do right on the Glorious Fourth, and he had kept his word. And what had been his reward? Wallets had been flaunted in his face; he had seen a score of excellent watches that could have been had for the taking; and now Detective Craddock intimated that Thubway Tham might not have kept his word after all. Rage seethed within him.

In a minute Craddock left the train. Thubway Tham rode on uptown.

He pressed nearer the two men he had been watching. He of the flashy clothes was engaged in conversation with the obese individual now, no doubt hoping to get an introduction to the two nieces.

"Great crowd, and great day!" he was saying. "Met one freak, though-funny little fellow who told me to watch out for pickpockets. What do you think of that?"

"Wherever there is a crowd you'll find some fellows who are afraid of pickpockets," the uncle replied. "I'd like to see one get my wallet!"

"Here, too! A man must be asleep to be robbed like that. These pickpockets with wonderful skill are found only in fiction."

Thubway Tham gnashed his teeth. He had forgotten his promises now; Temptation had won a victory. He pressed still closer and considered the possibilities.

Usually, Thubway Tham picked a pocket just as a station was reached and then stepped out of the train and hurried through the crowd. That made his work considerably safer. But here were two victims, and Tham disliked to commit double robberies. However, such remarks were not to be allowed to pass without punishment.

"The thilly thimpth!" Tham told himself. "It would be a crime to let them get away without bein' touched."

Tham decided to run the risk. He lurched against the obese individual at the right moment; his left hand darted down, and he became the possessor of uncle's wallet without the slightest trouble. Then he edged to the rear of the flashily dressed man. The train was nearing the station at Twenty-third Street.

Again Tham lurched forward, and the wallet of the flashily dressed person went into Tham's pocket. The doors slid open, and Tham stepped out onto the platform and then hurried up to the street. He emptied the wallets as quickly as possible and got rid of everything except the currency they had contained. So! Boasters are always punished, Tham thought.

Then he felt a tag at the tail of his coat. For an instant he was panic-stricken. Had his crime been observed? A vision of the big prison up the river flashed before him as he turned.

Before him stood the youngster he had entertained at Coney Island, and his smiling mother was behind him.

"Here he ith," the boy said.

"Well, did you have a good time?" Thubway Tham demanded. "Have a really Gloriouth Fourth?"

"Yes, t'ank you."

"Glad you did," said Thubway Tham, "When I wath a little boy, I never had many pleathant holidayth. Be a good boy and alwayth mind your mother, and then you'll be a good man."

"Yes, thir," the boy said. "You ith a good man, ain't you?"

Tham laughed and turned away. But that last remark of the boy's had struck home. Who was he to preach to a youngster? Why, he hadn't even kept his promise to himself and to Craddock. He had lifted two wallets just because he could not conquer anger and temptation!

"I am a crooked crook!" Thubway Tham told himself. "I am not even a dethent crook. It would therve me right if Craddock took me in, if he caught me with the goodth. And me talkin' to that little boy!"

Tham felt self-abasement for the first time in years.

"I thaid I would not thteal a thing on the Gloriouth Fourth, and I broke my word!" he mumbled. "I am a thcoundrel!"

He removed his cap and scratched at his head. He felt very miserable about it. Breaking faith with Craddock was bad enough, but he had also broken faith with himself. That was worse.

"If a man can't even trutht himthelf, he ith in a bad way," Tham declared.

Then he glanced up at the clock on the big tower, preparatory to walking downtown in the cool air. The hands of the clock showed half an hour after midnight, exactly. Tham's face glowed; his eyes sparkled; and his heart was happy.

"I didn't break any promithe, either!" Tham told himself. "It wath not more than fifteen minuteth ago that I took thothe walletth. It wath on the fifth and not on the Gloriouth Fourth!"

As if that fact made a great difference in the quality of his crime, Thubway Tham began whistling a lively air as he walked briskly toward the southern end of Manhattan Island.

THUBWAY THAM'S HOLDUP

OF COURSE, and naturally, Thubway Tham had a multitude of acquaintances among those of the underworld. For the underworld of a city is a big family, like a circus, though there are many subdivisions. It is an ordinary thing for those In the same line of work to club together — burglars with burglars, pickpockets with pickpockets, second-story men with other second-story men, and so on.

Thubway Tham was different in some things, however. He was a sort of acknowledged leader among the pickpockets, a past master, a man who was important enough to have his certain district and to command there. He worked only in the subway during rush hours, and others of his ilk refrained from plying their nefarious profession there. And so Thubway Tham to a certain extent felt called upon to treat other dips as inferiors. He was gentle with them when he met them, but he always gave the impression that they were semiprofessionals at best.

Being a king of a certain branch of the underworld, in a manner of speaking, Thubway Tham now and then indulged in conversation with other royalty. Thus it happened that, on a certain day, he spent some time in talk with one "Shifty" Shane, a well-known holdup man.

Shifty Shane was an acknowledged king himself. Many a gentleman who had been relieved of roll and watch at the point of a gun had been honored with the attention of Shifty Shane, though he did not know it. Certain police officers suspected things regarding Shifty Shane, but seemed powerless to catch him "with the goods." Shifty Shane had been arrested on suspicion so many times, and always had walked forth a free man, that he had begun to look upon such a thing as a part of his regular existence.

Shifty even worked, had a certain job, so that he could not be placed in durance vile on a charge of having no visible means of support. Thubway Tham admired Shifty Shane in a way, as one king might admire another. They both were "getting away with it," for Thubway Tham had aroused the police department to such an extent that a special detective, Craddock by name, had been detailed to watch him.

So, upon this memorable day, Thubway Tham and Shifty Shane held conversation in the rear of a little, greasy restaurant where they had been eating the morning meal. There being nobody else in the immediate vicinity, the talk turned to professional matters. Thubway Tham related how he had fooled Detective Craddock and had plucked a fat wallet from the pocket of a man in a subway train. Shifty Shane modestly admitted that he was sole author and executor of a particularly notorious holdup that had been detailed at length in the public press.

Following these tales, Thubway Tham and Shifty Shane began considering their different branches of crime, each contending that his was by far the superior and called for the greater skill.

"Why, you thilly ath!" Thubway Tham made bold to exclaim. "You would not latht ath long ath a thnowball in a furnathe if you tried my game! You would have about ath much chance of gettin' away with it ath a white blackbird eatin' a red-hot thnowball and freethin' to death! It taketh thkill, you thimp! A man hath to have trained handth. Thee?"

"Like that, huh?" inquired Shifty Shane. "And I suppose, Tham, old scout, that you imagine a holdup man has a cinch."

"Of courthe he hath!" Tham told him. "He thtepth from behind thomething and poketh a gun in the fathe of a man and goeth through him before the thimp getth over bein' thcared. I don't uthe a gun, I uthe thkill only. Thkill and thienthe! That ith me!"

"I could pick pockets all day long and get away with it. I think it's a woman's work, if you ask me," Shifty Shane remarked, sitting closer to the table.

"I am not athkin' you," said Thubway Tham, "but it ith not woman'th work, juth the thame. A dip mutht know how to read men. He mutht not pick a man who ith tho nervouthe that he ith alwayth lookin' for thomething to happen. He mutht be thure that nobody elthe theeth him work, and when he doeth work he mutht do it mighty quick."

"But it don't take any nerve," Shifty Shane objected. "And it does take nerve to poke a gun into a man's face and make him elevate his paws.

You never know what the simp is going to do. He might wilt, and again he might come up shootin'. A scared man is liable to do anything. I know what I'm talkin' about; Tham. I've had a few close calls."

"Maybe tho,'" Tham said. "But I don't think much of the game. It doeth not call for thkill and thienthe."

"Well, it calls for nerve, believe me," Shifty Shane repeated. "It calls for more nerve than dippin' a hand into a gent's pocket, and don't you forget it."

"It ith nothin' to hold up a man," Tham declared.

"I suppose you think you could do it."

"Hold up a man? It ith about the eathietht thing I know," Tham told him. "It ith like takin' candy from a baby."

"Oh, is that so?" retorted Shifty Shane with a sneer.

"Thertainly it ith tho!" said Tham.

"And you could do it?"

"Eathy!"

"I've got a hundred dollars you can't," Shifty Shane replied, bending over the table. "I've got a little hundred in my kick right now, old boy, that I gathered in night before last from a gentleman who had stayed out too late and was weaving his way home about three in the morning. I'm willing to bet that little hundred, you poor dip, that you can't go out tonight and pull off a holdup and get away with it. And if you don't make the bet you're a bluff!"

"Well, my goodneth!" Tham exclaimed. "I thertainly don't know any eathier way of rnakin' a hundred dollarth. You mutht want to get rid of that money mighty bad."

"Yes?"

"Yeth!" said Thubway Tham. "You jutht tell me all about thith bet. Underthand?"

"You got a mask and a gun?"

"Good heaventh, no!" said Thubway Tham. "I don't uthe them in my buthimeth."

"Well, I'll lend 'em to you," said Shifty Shane. "And I'll trot along behind and watch you do the work. But I'm tellin' you right now that you'll probably either be shot or taken to the jug."

"Yeth?"

"Yes. You'll find out, old boy, that a holdup is no cinch. It takes nerve."

"You thaid that before," Tham reminded him. "Nerve ith my middle name."

"Then we make the bet?"

"Yeth," said Thubway Tham. "You may kith that hundred dollarth farewell, Thifty Thane."

II.

MINOR details being settled, Thubway Tham and Shifty Shane parted, walking in opposite directions after they left the restaurant, both knowing that it would do them no particular good to have some police officer see them together.

Thubway Tham had been brave during the discussion, but he did not feel so brave now. It was the newness of the thing that bothered him; he never had held up a man before. But he tried to tell himself that he could do anything Shifty Shane could do, and also that he wanted to win that hundred dollars. Tham's funds were not so ample that he could afford to toss a hundred up in the air and not even look to see where the wind blew it.

So Tham determined to go through with the business and trust to luck. It had been a fool bet, he told himself, but he could not afford to back out now. And, whether he won or lost, he would make another bet of the same amount — that Shifty Shane could not pick a pocket and get away with the swag.

He would force Shifty Shane to agree, or term him a bluff.

Turning a corner, Thubway Tham came face to face with Detective Craddock.

"If it isn't my old friend, Tham!" Craddock exclaimed.

"My goodneth!" Tham retorted. "Jutht ath I wath feelin' extra good, I thee your ugly fathe! There ith no joy in life any more."

"How is everything, Tham?"

"Everything wath fine until I thaw you!"

"Been gathering in any wallets lately?"

"Thay!" Tham exclaimed. "That ith no way to talk. Jutht becauthe onthe I wath thent up for pickin' a pocket —"

"Lay off the comedy, Tham. I guess that we understand each other," Craddock told him. "Are you thinking of taking a little ride in our subway today?"

"Thuppothe I am?"

"In which case, Tham, I'll be compelled to trot right along with you and see what you do," Craddock told him. "Several peevish gentlemen have visited police headquarters recently to relate that their wallets have been stolen while they were riding in the subway."

"Why pick on me?" Tham asked. "You may thearth me —"

"A fat lot of good that would do me!" said Detective Craddock. "But, as I have told you a couple of hundred times, I am going to get you one of these fine days, old boy, and I am going to get you right, catch you with the goods, and have the pleasure of hearing some judge remark that you are to be incarcerated for about eight years."

"Yeth?"

"Yes!" said Craddock. "You have been a lucky bird, Tham, old boy, but one of these days you are going to make a slip, and then it will be curtains for you."

"If I made a thlip right in front of your nothe, you thilly ath, you couldn't thee it!" Tham told him angrily. "All you do ith jutht pethter the life out of me. Every time thomebody lotheth hith roll in the thubway, you blame me."

"Naturally," Craddock said.

"And it ith not right! Am I the only man in thith town?"

"The only one, so far as we know, who makes a specialty of lifting wallets in the subway," Craddock answered.

"There may be thome thingth," remarked Thubway Tham, "that you do not know."

"No doubt, no doubt — but I know a few," Craddock retorted. "How about it? You going to take a little subway ride?"

"Look at me and thee," Tham told him.

He turned his back upon the grinning detective and walked up the street. He stepped out rapidly, darting cleverly through the crowd, and

Craddock was forced to use all his ingenuity to keep him in sight. That made the detective feel certain that Tham intended to dodge him and dart into some subway entrance.

But Tham, it appeared, was in no great hurry to do so. He walked north as far as Union Square, and looked at the big battleship replica there as if he never had seen it before. He entered a cigar store and purchased some cigarettes, and lighted one and walked on up the street. Now and then he turned into some cross street and journeyed a block or so, and always Craddock followed, knowing full well that Thubway Tham was trying to make him angry. Craddock knew that, in a game of wits, the man who grows angry is lost, so he fought against his rising temper.

Finally Tham did enter the subway, and caught a train for downtown. Craddock got into the same car, but Tham made no attempt to steal a purse. Far downtown he left the train and went to one of his pet haunts, where he sat down at a table in the rear of the room. Then he looked up at Craddock and grinned.

"I thrutht that you liked your exerthithe," said Thubway Tham.

"Never mind, Tham — I'll get you yet!"

"I have my doubtth," Tham said. "I think you are wathtin' time, if you athk me."

Craddock left the resort, and Tham, refusing to hold conversation with any of his acquaintances, sat at the table and thought of the bet he had made with Shifty Shane. Once more he told himself that he had been a fool to take up such a bet — and once more he repeated that he could do anything a man like Shifty Shane could do.

"It ith only a kid'th trick!" he told himself.' "Thtickin' gun in a man'th fathe ith no job for a thkillful gent. But I mutht go through with it now, I thuppothe."

He did not intend to ply his own trade in the subway that day. He had merely been playing with Detective Craddock. Tham intended to keep his nerves cool for the adventure of the night. He would hold up a man and win Shifty Shane's hundred dollars, and then he would tease Shifty into betting a hundred that he could pick a pocket.

Tham tried to remember to consider everything. He would not dress in the usual fashion, he decided; he would put on a dark suit of clothes and a dark cap. He would try to walk in a manner that was unusual to him. If his victim sent in a description to the police, Thubway Tham did not want that description to recall him to the minds of the detectives. It was bad enough, he decided, to be watched all the time as a pickpocket without getting notoriety as a possible holdup man, too.

And then, there was his lisp. He would have to be very careful about that. It would "give him away" quicker than anything else; he didn't want to run the chance of trying to convince the officers that somebody had lisped in imitation of him to cast suspicion in his direction. The officers might not believe it.

So he decided that he would use words that would not cause him to lisp. He could not even say "Hands up!" without lisping. He thought of several phrases that he would have to employ, and he invented some that would do. He decided, too, that he would speak in a low, gruff voice.

"It ith goin' to be a thinthe," he told himself finally. "All the thame, it wath a foolith bet and I ain't goin' to ever make another like it. Life ith too thort!"

He left the resort — to find that Craddock was standing on the corner, waiting for him.

"Thay! Don't you ever work?" Thubway Tham demanded. "You hang around me like a dog after a thteak. I theem to be mighty popular with you."

"You are, Tham, you are!" Detective Craddock assured him. "I don't know anybody I'd rather be around just now. I love to keep my eyes on you, Tham, old boy."

"Yeth?"

"Yes, Tham, old scout. I have an ambition to gratify, you know; I want to see you sent up."

"If you live to thee that," said Thubway Tham, "you are goin' to die at a ripe old age."

"So?"

"Tho!" Tham exclaimed. "And now I don't want you to pethter me any more. I am not goin' into the thubway thith afternoon, if it ith any of your buthineth."

"Word of honor, Tham?" Craddock asked.

"Yeth, thir!"

"That satisfies me, Tham," Craddock told him. "You may be a dip, but you always keep your word. I'm gratified, Tham. I've got some other business that needs my attention, and this will give me a chance to work at it."

Without another word, Detective Craddock turned around and started up the street. He was an officer of the law, and Thubway Tham was a former convict and a known pickpocket, but there was a certain code of honor between them. They were playing a desperate game, but they played it according to rules and regulations.

And Craddock did have other business that required his attention. He had orders to investigate in a certain district where there had been many holdups recently!

III.

HAVING dined, Thubway Tham retired to the room he called home and dressed in a dark suit and put on a dark cap. Then he left the cheap lodging house by means of the rear stairs, slipped through the dark alley until he reached the next street, glanced up and down to make sure that there was no officer in sight who knew him, and then hurried to a certain corner where he had a rendezvous with Shifty Shane.

This rendezvous was some blocks away, and Thubway Tham had plenty of time to think while he walked.

"There ith nothin' to it!" he told himself. "I am jutht a bit nervouth becauthe it ith all tho new to me. It ith only a coward'th trick to hold up a man, and I thertainly can do it: I'll thow thith Thifty Thane, and then I'll thow him that my buthineth ith twithe arth hard. The thimp!"

Shifty was waiting for him at the dark corner, and Thubway Tham followed him into an alley and down it until they came to a heap of old packing cases.

"I'm playing a square game with you, Tham, old scout, and I sincerely hope you won't be shot or jugged," Shifty Shane told him. "I'm goin' to put you wise to the game as much as I can before you start out."

"Thankth," Tham told him. "In the first place, Tham, always get the jump on your man. Be at him before he knows there is anybody around, and jam the muzzle of your gat at him so that it will look as big as a cannon. Give him his orders and frisk him before he gets over his scare. Then push him away from you, and make your getaway as good as you can."

"Thankth," Tham said again. "That theemth like a lot of inthtruction for thuch a little job."

"Don't make the mistake of thinkin' this is a little job, Tham. You're goin' up against a he-man's game, remember. You'll probably shiver in your shoes before you're through."

"I don't fancy I'll thiver much," Tham said. "You got that hundred with you?"

"I've got it — don't worry. But I'm not goin' to pay it to you, Tham. Nope! I can tell right now from the way you're actin' that you're goin' to fall down, and fall down hard! You're scared, boy — scared."

"Ith that tho?" Thubway Tham retorted with a sneer. "It ith nothin' to thcare a man to thtep from a dark thpot and jam a gun at another man. You'd know how to be thcared if you ever nipped a wallet in a jammed thubway car with a hundred perthonth lookin' on."

"I could pick pockets from sunrise to sunset and never get a thrill," declared Shifty Shane. "It's an old woman's game, always was and always will be."

"You," Thubway Tham declared happily, "could not thnitch a thingle wallet and get away with it. And I've got a hundred dollarth that thayth you can't."

"Who — me? If I was in that game I'd do all my day's work before I went to breakfast," Shifty said. "And I'd nick some real wallets, believe me — no small fry stuff."

"I've got a hundred dollarth that thayth you can't nick one," Thubway Tham told him again. "I'll make a bet, like you did with me. If you don't make it, you're a bluff. Thee?"

"You're on, old-timer," Shifty Shane told him. "But one thing at a time. You've got a stunt to do tonight."

"You can try to nick that wallet durin' ruth hour tomorrow," Tham explained. "I'll do the thquare thing — put you withe to a lot about the game."

"Thanks, but I won't need any information," Shifty said. "There's nothing to know about a game like that. Come along, now, and let's see how you can handle a he-man's game."

Shifty Shane led the way down the semi-dark street, and Thubway Tham, on the opposite side, followed him half a block in the rear. They went through a district of cheap shops and warehouses, and came to a residence section. Here were the homes of substantial men who often loitered late in their officers to increase their incomes.

Shifty Shane stepped into the mouth of an alley, and Thubway Tham, making sure that he was not observed, followed him swiftly.

"Right here is where I nipped a guy the other night," Shifty Shane explained. "You'll notice that the light on the corner shines so that it is in your man's eyes to a certain extent. Them little things count, Tham, in a game like this. Spot your guy as he comes along from the car line, step out and get the drop on him at just the right time, get it over with, make him move on, and then run through this dark alley. Understand?"

"I grathp you," said Tham.

"We'll walk through the alley now so you'll be sure of your footin'. It's a little early, anyway."

They walked through the alley and back again so that Thubway Tham knew the ground well and could make a swift getaway if it proved necessary. But Tham kept telling himself it would not be necessary at all. He was beginning to lose some of his fear.

"I'm goin' to walk on down the street to the next corner," said Shifty Shane. "I can watch you work from there. After you make the getaway, we'll meet where I said, and you can tell your little story. Understand?"

"I grathp you," Tham said again.

Without another word, Shifty Shane left the alley and walked briskly down the street like a belated pedestrian hurrying to his home and family. Thubway Tham watched until he knew that Shane had secluded himself in the darkness there, and then he glanced up the street in the opposite direction, from whence his victim was to come.

"Thilly ath of a thtunt!" Tham told himself. "It ith no he-man'th game at all! It ith takin' advantage. No man ith goin' to thtart a row when another hath a gun on him. I thould thay not!"

Pedestrians did not appear to be numerous. Thubway Tham watched the walk carefully. There were two or three places between the alley and the corner where shafts of light cut across the walk, and Tham knew he would have a chance to estimate his man as he walked by those streaks of light.

After a time, he saw a man coming from the car line. He was a large-sized man, and held packages in his arms, and walked with a swinging stride. Thubway Tham observed him closely. And then, he told himself, he "had a hunch."

Tham couldn't explain the hunch, but he declared to himself that it was not a case of common fear. However, he retreated into the alley until he was in pitch darkness and could not be seen from the walk, and there he crouched while the man went by and continued on his way. Then he went back to the mouth of the alley.

The thought came to Thubway Tham that perhaps he had been a fool. Shifty Shane, watching at the lower corner, had seen that man pass — evidently a prosperous gentleman hurrying home, with his arms full of bundles. What better incentive for a holdup man?

He feared that Shifty Shane might laugh at him and demand an explanation. Shane might even accuse him of cowardice.

"I gueth I'll have to get the next man," Tham told himself, and kept a close watch.

In time, another man came rapidly down the walk. Thubway Tham affixed the mask Shifty Shane had given him, and took Shane's revolver from his pocket.

"Aw, it ith eathy!" Tham told himself.

He crouched just at the corner of the alley wall. He waited until his victim was the proper distance away. And then he sprang out suddenly and threw up his revolver.

"Put 'em up!" he commanded gruffly.

Then Thubway Tham happened upon one of those surprises that disconcert a holdup man. The victim's hands came up — but one of them came up shooting!

Often during his life, Thubway Tham had been surprised, as upon the day, years before, when he had been caught taking a watch from a man's pocket. But never before had he been so astonished as he was now. The victim was no craven who would accept the word of a holdup man that he must give up his money or his life. This victim was not acting according to the code.

Thubway Tham gave a screech and dived into the welcome, black mouth of the alley. He heard the shout of his intended victim that he halt or take the consequences. But Thubway Tham did not think of halting.

He shed the mask as he ran, and he dropped Shifty Shane's weapon. Thubway Tham was a little man, and had speed; but he did not run this night – he flew. Somehow, it never occurred to him to shoot in return. Being a pickpocket and nothing more, he never had resorted to weapons and was not familiar with them. He did not even know whether he was a good shot, and he did not intend finding out by firing at a target that fired in reply.

Down the dark alley he dashed, thankful that Shifty Shane had shown him the getaway route. Behind him spoke the revolver of the man who had been picked as victim. He was pursuing, and still was calling upon Thubway Tham to halt or take the consequences.

Tham did not intend to do either if it could be avoided. He came to a low fence Shifty Shane had designated, vaulted it, ran through a rear yard and so reached a dark street. He doubled back toward the main street, keeping in the shadows. His heart was pounding at his ribs, his breath was coming in gasps, and he was trying now to run noiselessly. He doubted whether he fever would gain the rendezvous, but he did. There he rested, panting, and waited for Shane.

"It wath a thilly trick!" he muttered. "It therveth me jutht right! It ith a kid'th trick thtickin' up a man like that, and nobody but a coward would do it!"

Ten minutes later Shifty Shane put in an appearance.

"Well, Tham, as a holdup man, you're a bird!" he declared. "I'd have been here sooner, but I had to stop and laugh five or ten minutes. Understand?"

"Tho?" said Thubway Tham. "It wath no time to laugh."

"You must have gone at him like a rank amateur, boy. You must have given him plenty of time to bring his artillery up from the rear."

"He didn't need any time," Thubway Tham replied. "He theemed to be expectin' it and to be ready."

"How about that hundred, old boy?"

"Here it ith," said Tham, handing it over. "It ith no man'th game, anyway, thtickin' up another man."

"I guess you know now that it takes nerve, all right."

"Maybe tho," said Tham. "You wait until tomorrow noon when you try to lift a wallet. You'll know what taketh nerve, then!"

IV.

THE FOLLOWING morning, Thubway Tham found himself still angry and a trifle frightened. It was no great pleasure to have a man empty a revolver at you, and at the same time pursue you with the intention of effecting a capture and sending you to prison for a long term.

"What a thimp I wath!" Tham told himself, as he dressed. "And it cotht me jutht a hundred dollarth to find out that I wath a thimp."

Then he remembered his other bargain with Shifty Shane, and smiled.

"Here ith where I get thquare with him," Tham mused. "He can never lift a wallet and get away with it in a thouthand yearth. Here ith where I get hith goat!"

Tham met Shifty Shane, as per arrangement, in a certain restaurant and after they had breakfasted they got down to business.

"Still lookin' a little white around the gills," Shifty Shane told him.

"Yeth? You wait!" said Tham.

"I'm not worryin' any about this stunt, old-timer. Snitchin' a wallet is about the easiest thing in the world, if you ask me. It's a kid's job, all right for a youngster just breakin' in — that's all. Nothin' easier."

"Jutht you wait," Tham told him. "Now you let me give you thome advithe. When you get into a crowded car, firtht pick your man. Get one who lookth ath if he had a fat wallet and who lookth ath if he had hith mind on buthineth or thomethin' like that."

"You're wastin' time, boy. I don't need advice."

"You better lithen jutht the thame," Tham told him. "Get a man who carrieth hith wallet in a hip pocket, if you can find one. There ith a few boobth like that thtill left on earth, and motht of them are in New York. Jutht ath you get to a thtation, bruth againtht him and do your work. Be thure nobody elthe theeth you. If there ith a roar, drop the wallet the firtht thing. Thee?"

"I knew all that thtuff when I wath two yearth old," said Shifty Shane, deliberately mocking Thubway and thereby incurring a measure of sudden hatred.

"If you are one of thethe birdth that can't learn anything, I have no more to thay!" Tham told him angrily.

They completed their arrangements and appointed another rendezvous, and then they left the restaurant, Shifty Shane following a short distance behind Thubway Tham.

Tham wanted Shane to fail; he wanted the hundred dollars back; but he 3id not want a fellow criminal to be caught — not because he loved this particular fellow criminal, but because he was against the police first, last and always. So he watched to make sure that no detective he knew trailed them.

Tham saw nobody who appeared to be dangerous to their liberty, and therefore, after a time, he led the way into a subway entrance near City Hall.

They boarded an uptown train that was jammed with passengers, and squeezed into a car. Thubway Tham got a short distance from Shifty Shane and prepared to watch him work. A glance showed him that no officer he knew was in the car.

It happened that a prosperous-looking gentleman stood at Shifty Shane's elbow. He looked like the sort of man who would carry a well-filled wallet, and he seemed to be thinking of business affairs or something equally engrossing. Shifty Shane got as near as possible to his intended victim. He had decided to lift the wallet at the first station. By pressing against the man's body, he could feel a wallet in a hip pocket.

Shifty turned his head, and from his eyes to those of Thubway Tham there flashed a message. Tham relayed one back to the effect that he was wise, had his eyes open, and would watch Shifty's work.

Shane turned around again. He knew that the train would be at the station in a moment. Some of the passengers were preparing to squeeze toward the door.

Then Shifty Shane felt a lump come into his throat. He had declared that lifting a wallet was child's play, but he did not think it now. He imagined a thousand things that might happen as soon as he made the attempt. Terror shook him; he wondered whether Thubway Tham guessed what he was experiencing.

Tham did. He had experienced something similar, in years long past, when he had lifted his first wallet. He knew what Shifty Shane was feeling.

The train pulled into the station and stopped. The victim left the car, and so did Shifty Shane, and so did Thubway Tham. The latter followed Shane to the street, and spoke to him one block away, when he was certain that he was not being observed.

"Get a fat one?" Tham asked.

"Couldn't work it," Shane explained, wiping the perspiration from his forehead. "I had that bird all ready to pluck, and the last second he happened to turn and look me straight m the eyes."

"That ith tough luck," said Tham. He knew that Shane was telling a falsehood. "I thuppothe you'll have to try again. You go ahead and I'll be right behind."

Shane walked several blocks down the street. He didn't want to go into the subway again. He told himself that a man should stick to his own trade. Why had he been such a fool as to make that wager with Thubway Tham?

But he couldn't get out of it now, Tham had done his part, and Shifty Shane would have to do his or prove himself a craven. He gathered his courage and plunged into the subway entrance nearest him.

Thubway Tham followed. Shane caught a downtown train, and Tham got into the car behind him and went down the aisle a short distance. Then he turned arount to watch Shifty Shane, and, instead, faced Detective Craddock!

"My goodneth! Here you are again!" Tham said, to hide his sudden terror.

"Walked right in, didn't you?" Craddock asked. "Sorry you turned and saw me — probably would have caught you if you hadn't."

Craddock bent close and whispered the words. Thubway Tham turned an innocent face toward him.

"I give you my word of honor," he said, "that when I got on thith train I had no idea of — er — workin'."

"That right, Tham?"

"Yeth, thir!"

"I suppose I'll have to believe you — you always keep your word. But it makes me a trifle nervous to see you in a crowded subway car, Tham, old boy."

"I wath uptown, and had to get downtown, didn't I?" Tham asked. "You can thearch me, and you can watch me —"

"Not necessary just now, Tham," said Craddock, grinning. "I don' think you'll try anything while I'm standing at your side."

"That would not thtop me if I wanted to work," Tham said. "But I do not want to work."

"Say!" Craddock exclaimed. "What does this sudden reformation mean? You didn't work yesterday, and you aren't today. Fallen heir to a fortune, or something like that?"

"No, thir. I am jutht behavin' mythelf," Thubway Tham told him.

During this conversation with Detective Craddock, Tham had been observing Shifty Shane. The latter had picked a victim, and Tham knew by his manner that he intended making a genuine attempt this time. And Craddock, the particular foe of all pickpockets of the city, was in the car.

Tham continued the conversation, and meanwhile his wits were at work. He didn't want Craddock to catch Shifty Shane, who would not even turn around so that he could be given a signal. Moreover, Shane knew Craddock. If he turned and saw Craddock, he would be saved; if he did not —

Tham knew that the train was nearing a station and that Shifty Shane would make the attempt. If he succeeded everything would be all right, but if he bungled the job there would be an uproar. Craddock was standing within fifteen feet of Shifty Shane.

Thubway Tham replied to the detective's questions carefully, and tried to think of a way of saving Shane, but he could not. He began to have a great fear that Shane was going to bungle the job. He had another "hunch." Turning his face away from Shane and toward Craddock, he began talking hard, getting all the detective's attention.

"I want a good job," he said. "I want to go thtraight, but you copth won't let me. You know how old I am. I am almotht forty."

"Slowing up, are you, and want to get out of the game?" Craddock asked. "I know what you're trying to do, Tham. You're trying to turn straight so I'll never realize my ambition. You're getting scared of me."

"My goodneth! If I am thcared of you, I mutht be a poor thtick!" Tham told him. "You ain't got thuch a record. I thaid what I thaid, and it wath the truth. I did not thuppothe you'd believe it. Ath!"

Craddock laughed lightly. At the same moment, the train slowed down for the station. Tham did not look toward Shifty Shane; he kept his blazing eyes on Craddock's face and held his gaze. But Thubway Tham was almost praying.

The train stopped; the doors slid open.

"I mean to thay —" Tham began.

A sudden bedlam interrupted him.

"Pickpocket! Thief!" shrieked some woman near the doorway.

Thubway Tham experienced mingled emotions. That cry meant that Shifty Shane had failed, for which Tham was glad; but it meant also that Shane was in grave danger, for which Tham was sorry.

Craddock gripped him by the arm and whirled to look. Tham looked, too. There was a turmoil in the doorway and on the station platform. People entering the car and people, trying to leave were colliding. Tham saw that Shifty Shane had darted away from danger and was walking slowly toward the exit.

Taking Tham along with him, Craddock thrust through the crowd to the door.

"I saw him reaching in that gentleman's pocket," a woman was declaring. "He took out a purse — there it is on the floor. He turned through the door and into the crowd. He was a big, blond man —"

Tham felt relieved. The woman had made the mistake nine persons out of ten will make after one hurried glance — had given a wrong description. Shifty Shane was an ordinary-sized man and had black hair.

Craddock took names and addresses and announced that he would make a report. The gentleman regained his wallet. Then Craddock went out on the platform with Thubway Tham, and the train roared on.

"He made a getaway, I suppose," Craddock said. "I'll get blazes for this. Tham, did you see any pickpocket in that car? I want the truth!"

"I give you my word of honor," said Thubway Tham, "that I thaw no dip on that car!"

He meant it, and Craddock knew that he meant it. For Thubway Tham did not consider Shane a dip, but a holdup man.

"And I thuppothe that it ith a mighty good thing for me that I wath away from that door and talkin' to you," he continued. "It ith a wonder you do not accuthe me."

"No chance this time, Tham."

"Maybe you'd better thearch me at that," Tham said.

"Aw, shut up!" Craddock exclaimed. He led the way to the street, and there he turned and contemplated Thubway Tham again.

"I'm getting mighty sick of this business!" he declared. "If it wasn't for the hope of catching you one of these days, I'd quit the force and get a different job."

"You mad about thomethmg?" Tham wanted to know.

"I'll make this report and get bawled out because I didn't catch that fellow, and the boss never will take into consideration that there was a big crowd and that the dip was out on the platform and away before that fool woman screeched."

"Well, it ith all in the game," Tham said.

"I'm getting a bit sick of the game. A man takes his life in his hands —"

"Well, my goodneth! How could a man take hith life in hith handth in a cathe like that?" Thubway Tham asked. "And you know, you thimp, that no regular dip carrieth a gun, anyway."

"Aw, shut up! I'm not talking about that just now. I almost got mine last night."

"How wath that?"

"There've been a lot of holdups recently in a certain district and I went down there last night to try to get a line on somebody. I was ready for action, too. The stickup man sprang on me, and I came up shooting.

But he didn't have any nerve. He ducked through an alley and made a get-away — didn't even shoot back. If he had I might have got mine."

"My goodneth!" Tham gasped. "Where was all thith?"

Craddock told him — and Thubway Tham knew.

THREE-QUARTERS of an hour later, Tham collected one hundred dol-lars from a trembling Shifty Shane.

"Every man to hith job," Tham told him, "You leave the thubway to me and go right ahead thtickin' up pedethianth. Thee? I knew you'd fall down."

"Well, you fell down last night!" Shane retorted.

"There wath a differenthe," Thubway Tham told him. "That man I tackled latht night — I recognized him jutht ath I told him to hold up hith handth. He wath Detective Craddock, and you know that he ith after me. If you don't believe it you look in the evenin' paperth — they all thay how Craddock almotht caught a holdup man at that alley. Tho I had a reathon!"

Part of it was a lie, of course — Tham had not recognized Craddock. But Tham felt that a good pickpocket was entitled to put it over on a common holdup man when opportunity offered.

THUBWAY THAM
AND MR. CLACKWORTHY

IT IS taken for granted that you are fairly well acquainted with Mr. Amos Clackworthy, the swindler extraordinary regarding whose nefarious practices much has been written, and also with "The Early Bird," Mr. Clackworthy's expressive and unusual assistant.

Many chronicles have been written concerning the operations of this precious pair in the town of Chicago, which is a provincial village on the shore of Lake Michigan, not far from Gary, Indiana, and a short distance east of Elgin, Illinois. Most good complete maps show it.

The chronicler, naturally, being a friend of Mr. Amos Clackworthy and The Early Bird and possibly in sympathy with their mode of existence, has cast over them the glamor of romance. And it is true that, in the town of Chicago, they have been able to profit handsomely through their craft and cunning.

But this is the story of what happened when Mr. Amos Clackworthy and The Early Bird took a journey to New York City and met divers and sundry characters there — notably Thubway Tham!

I.

MR. AMOS Clackworthy peered through the window of the compartment in his usual dignified manner and observed the congested district of the city as the train rushed on toward the magnificent and justly famous terminal.

As a usual thing the countenance of Mr. Amos Clackworthy was inscrutable, but now he allowed just the hint of a smile to show in his face. A close observer might have said, also, that Mr. Clackworthy was slightly amused and was attempting to hide the fact.

The Early Bird had his face glued to the other window of the compartment, his nose almost flattened against the pane. The same close observer probably would have remarked that The Early Bird, if experiencing any emotions whatever, was a bit nervous as they approached their destination. Mr. Clackworthy glanced across at him casually and almost indulged in a smile. Finally he cleared his throat and spoke.

"New York!" he said in impressive tones. "James, it is a great city! A wonderful city! And yet, to my mind, it does not compare favorably with Chicago."

"Huh! Then whatcha comin' here for?" The Early Bird wanted to know. "The little village by Lake Mich was good enough for me. I wasn't hankerin' t' travel any!"

"After our short stay in New York you'll be able to appreciate Chicago all the more, James," Mr. Clackworthy assured him. "I have a little business to transact in New York. And I have brought you along because I am both pleased and amused with your companionship. Also, I may have need of you."

"Yeah?" The Early Bird queried. "I'm at home in old Chi, an' I'm willin' t' tackle anything there. But nix in this burg!"

"You appear to have some slight feeling of — shall we say fear?" Mr. Clackworthy remarked.

"I ain't longin' t' mingle much with the New York dicks," The Early Bird assured him instantly. "Not any! Some o' them birds have good memories."

"Do you intend me to gather that, some time in the dim past, you were a transgressor in this city?"

"Yeah, if you wanta put it that way," The Early Bird replied.

"And how long ago was it, James?"

"Ain'tcha gettin' personal, boss? About ten years."

"Um!" Mr. Clackworthy grunted, glancing through the window once more and observing the crowded streets. "And what was the precise nature of your transgression? Nothing, I certainly hope, that might call for a trip to the electric chair!"

"Huh? Not me. I never croaked anybody!" The Early Bird responded.

"Then — ?" Mr. Clackworthy questioned as one who has the right to know.

"I was whatcha call an all-around man," The Early Bird testified with his usual modesty. "I wasn't strong on the specialist stuff. I used t' play the dip sometimes."

"James! Don't mention it!"

"An' stickup man!"

"I am grieved to hear it, James," Mr. Clackworthy said. "Burglary is bad enough, but those lines of human endeavor you have mentioned are of the lowest order, to say the least. James, you were almost a common thug!"

"Yeah, I'm admittin' that," said The Early Bird.

"Of course, when I took you to be my assistant, I knew that you had been following nefarious ways. However, was there any specific crime more brazen than the others, something that would remain in the memories of officers of the law? Surely not, else they would have picked you up in Chicago long ago. I think that you have nothing to fear, James. Try to control your — let us say, your nervousness."

"Yeah, I'll make a stab at it, boss, but it's sure goin' t' be a hard job," The Early Bird replied frankly. "I never did entertain much good feelin' for these New York dicks and plain-clothes men. Don'tcha ever let anybody tell you they ain't wise birds!"

"There are many degrees of wisdom," Mr. Clackworthy observed, smiling slightly.

"Yeah, and some o' these New York dicks have taken every degree," The Early Bird replied firmly and with evident conviction. "I'm tellin' you they're wise old birds! I ain't hankerin' t' fuss with any o' 'em."

You have nothing to fear, James," Mr. Clackworthy assured him again. "We are coming into the station. Kindly see that our luggage is ready."

They walked along the platform with the crowd, went up into the terminal building, and started toward the taxi-cab entrance. Mr. Clackworthy appeared dignified and bored, as though a trip to New York was something he experienced twice weekly. The Early Bird, juggling two bags and a suitcase, glanced furtively here and there and had nothing to say.

"Mr. Clackworthy!"

The voice was deep and confident, and Mr. Clackworthy stopped instantly when he heard it, and turned. The Early Bird put down the luggage and turned also, and gulped. The first glance was enough to tell The Early Bird that an officer of the law confronted them.

"Sir?" Mr. Clackworthy said.

"I'm Craddock, of headquarters!"

"Of headquarters?" Clackworthy asked, raising his brows as though much puzzled.

"Yes!" Craddock said snappily. "Police headquarters, to be exact. Ever hear of the place?"

"Pardon me, sir, but what business can you have with me?" Mr. Clackworthy wanted to know.

"Nothing at present, Clackworthy," Craddock replied. "I just wanted to say that our friends in Chicago saw you take the train and wired us that a reception committee might not be amiss."

"This is an unexpected pleasure!" Mr. Clackworthy declared. "Is it not customary, however, for a gentleman to pay a visit to this city to attend to business without being bothered to accept the courtesies of a certain municipal department?"

"We don't bother gentlemen," said Craddock with considerable emphasis of deep meaning on the last word. He was a bit disconcerted by Clackworthy's sarcasm. "Just a tip, Clackworthy! Let your business in our fair city be of the legal variety. No high finance, Clackworthy! No cleverness! Eyes are watching you. That is all!"

"You are at liberty to watch me, sir," Clackworthy said.

"We certainly are," Craddock affirmed. "And how is Mr. James Early?" The Early Bird gulped and licked his lips. Mr. Clackworthy came to his rescue.

"Whatever James may have perpetrated in the past, he is now my man," Mr. Clackworthy said. "I vouch for him."

"Better get some man of proper standing to vouch for you, first," Detective Craddock told him. "Where do you intend to reside while you are honoring New York with this visit?"

Mr. Clackworthy named a hotel and assured the detective that reservations already had been made.

"Good enough!" Craddock said. "I'll not detain you any longer now. But watch your step, Clackworthy — watch your step! And you watch yours, Early. If you've reformed, you're in bad company!"

Detective Craddock turned his back deliberately and stalked away, but in departing, he winked at a plain-clothes man who, thereupon, began to shadow them. Craddock wanted to be sure that Clackworthy went to the hotel he had mentioned.

"I told you, boss," The Early Bird whispered. "I ain't hankerin' t' mix any with these New York dicks. That bird Craddock is a terror."

"Don't be alarmed," Mr. Clackworthy said. "The Chicago police, I suppose, sent the usual warning. They undoubtedly anticipate that I'll perpetrate some gigantic swindle, James, whereas this visit is an innocent one. I wish to invest some of my funds. Now we'll get our taxi-cab."

II.

THUBWAY THAM had made two round trips since morning from far downtown to Times Square. It was a dismal day. Tham was in need of funds, and on those two round trips he had not seen in the subway a single man who appeared to have wealth in a wallet concealed on his person.

At the end of the second round trip, Thubway Tham had gone to his room in the lodging house conducted by "Nosey" Moore to get from a dresser drawer a certain rabbit's foot supposed to hold the virtue of good fortune. Tham was of the opinion that, with this rabbit's foot in his pocket, his luck would change.

Descending the rickety stairs from the third to the second floor, Thubway Tham saw Mr. Moore behind the battered counter in the office, and the latter looked up and grinned when he saw Thubway Tham.

"Tham," said Mr. Moore, "how goes it?"

"Everything ith rotten!" Thubway Tham replied promptly.

"Poor crowd ridin' in the subway these days?" Mr. Moore wanted to know.

"I came back to get me my rabbit'th foot," Tham replied. "That ith the anthwer!"

"Bein' a dip has its bad moments," Mr. Moore observed with the air of a philosopher. "The big boys are the ones who cash in."

"What do you mean by the big boyth?" Tham asked.

"The smooth, clever swindlers, old-timer," Moore replied. "The men who look like church deacons and deal in thousands. Those are the lads who cop the big rolls these days. They talk like a book and they've got a front."

"Uh-huh!" Tham said. "I'm thatithfied when thingth are goin' right."

"One of those big boys came to town yesterday," said Moore.

"How ith that?"

"I had the word slipped to me an hour or so ago. His name is Amos Clackworthy, and he's a smooth article. Comes from Chicago."

"He might be thmooth in Thicago," Tham observed, "and pretty rough in New York."

"Oh, he's smooth, all right! He's pulled off some pretty big things in his day. Talks like a dictionary and throws a big front. Lives at a swell hotel. I don't know what his game is here in New York, but I'll bet it's a good one. He's got Jim Early with him, too — The Early Bird."

"Who ith thith Early Bird?" Thubway Tham asked.

"He used to be around these parts about ten years ago, before you got to going strong," Mr. Moore explained. "He was just a youngster then. Got run out of town and went to Chicago."

"What wath hith particular line?" Tham asked.

"A little of everything. He was a dip and a stickup man, and a second-rate burglar. Now he's with this Clackworthy. They're workin' together, of course."

"Well, it ith nothin' in my young life," Thubway Tham declared.

"You'll get mad if you ever meet this Clackworthy, Tham."

"How ith that?"

"Because he's always talkin' about low crooks," teased Nosey Moore, who always enjoyed Tham's indignation.

"Well, my goodneth! What ith he?"

"Oh, he thinks that he's a high-class, number one crook! He sneers at dips and stickup men and such, Tham. Says they're the lowest of the low." This was not perhaps entirely true but it was sure to arouse Tham's ire.

"My goodneth! He hateth himthelf, I thuppothe!"

"If you meet him, Tham, you'll get a laugh, if you're not made too mad."

"If I meet him and he thootth off hith mouth, I'll make him look like twenty thentth," Thubway Tham declared. "Thinkth that a dip ith the lowetht of the low, doeth he? Thinkth he ith tho thmart, doeth he? Huh! Nothey, I have theen thome of thethe thmart guyth before now. The thmarter they think they are, the harder they tumble!"

"Don't you let him sell you any oil stock, Tham."

"Do I look crathy?" Thubway Tham asked. "Ath it ith, I couldn't buy more than ten dollarth' worth. My roll ith tho flat that it ith no longer a roll. Thee you later, Nothey! I've got to go to work."

Thubway Tham descended the remainder of the distance to the street and directed his steps toward the nearest subway entrance. He promptly forgot about Mr. Amos Clackworthy and The Early Bird. Swindlers might swindle, as far as Thubway Tham was concerned. All he asked was that pickpockets remain away from the subway, which he had made his private ground of operations.

He caught an uptown express and got into a crowded car. The rabbit's foot was doing its work, Tham decided. This was the first crowded car he had encountered during the day, and in it were many well-dressed and prosperous-looking men.

Tham immediately began looking around for a possible victim, having ascertained first that there was no officer of his acquaintance near. Six feet in front of him he found his mark. He was a man of perhaps fifty, portly, red-faced, with the look of a prosperous broker about him. Thubway Tham decided that, in all probability, this gentleman carried a well-filled wallet, and Tham hoped that he had no more sense than to carry it in his hip pocket.

Working cautiously, Tham sought to lessen the space between his prospective victim and himself. It was slow work, because the aisle of the car was crowded. And suddenly Tham observed something else that caused him to pause.

Directly behind the man he had spotted stood another, a tall gentleman with a dignified appearance. Tham looked at him closely, wondering whether he would prove an easier victim. But he decided that the tall man probably made up in dignity what he lacked in ready funds. Even Tham was not infallible.

There was another thing that interested Tham, too. Beside this tall man was a smaller man, and Thubway Tham, glancing at him, knew him instantly for what he was — a crook. Tham wondered whether another was about to invade the sacred precincts of the subway for the purpose of lifting a leather. If so, he wanted to get ahead of the tall man and be in a position to press against the prosperous-looking man in front. But he found that he could not. He would have to wait, he decided, until the express had stopped at a couple of stations or so, and the crowd in the aisle had a chance to change.

The train approached a stop, and Thubway Tham prepared to edge forward when the doors slipped open. And then he saw something that appalled him. The man before him, whom he had identified as a crook, swung forward slowly and against the man Tham had picked for a victim!

What happened was so swift that none but Thubway Tham realized the truth. Thubway Tham had seen another poach on his preserves! This crook had not only dared to lift a leather in the subway, which all in the underworld left to Thubway Tham, but he had picked for his victim the very man Tham had spotted.

The train stopped, the doors slipped open, and the pickpocket stepped out to the crowded platform, followed by the tall man. Thubway Tham, anger surging within him, stepped out also. Then he saw that the tall man and the smaller man were companions, that they ascended to the street together. Thubway Tham followed.

He did not confront the pair at once. He knew them for strangers, and he wished to watch and listen for a moment before speaking. He followed at their heels through the crowd, into a side street, and managed to overhear some conversation.

"James," the tall man was saying, "I saw you pick that gentleman's pocket!"

"Yeah, a little expense coin, boss," The Early Bird replied.

"I believed that you had reformed to an extent, James," Mr. Clackworthy said. "And here you are descending to the level of a common dip again. You have not even thrown away the leather."

"Don'tcha worry, boss, I'll do it when we pass that trash can," The Early Bird replied.

"Do so, and then pick no more pockets. It is one of the lowest forms of crime, as I often have told you. A pickpocket, my dear James, is really beneath notice!"

Thubway Tham felt his blood boiling. A pickpocket was beneath notice, was he? And this pair ahead of him — why, they both were crooks, according to their talk! Thubway Tham took two quick steps forward and touched James Early on the arm. The Early Bird flinched. A touch on the arm, especially so short a time after he had picked a pocket, was enough to disconcert him, to say the least.

Mr. Amos Clackworthy stopped beside The Early Bird, and both regarded Thubway Tham in an unfriendly way.

"Thay!" Tham said, speaking in muffled tones from one corner of his mouth. "Who are you, and where are you from?"

"What's that t' you?" The Early Bird queried sneeringly.

"Jutht thith much! I thaw you lift that leather! You did it in the thubway, too. I wath jutht wonderin' whether you belong to thith town or are a thtranger."

"My dear sir —" Mr. Clackworthy began.

"Don't wathte your time throwin' that thort of talk toward me," Tham told him. "I'm withe to you birdth! You're crookth! That ith all right — I'm a dip mythelf."

"In that case —" Mr. Clackworthy made another attempt to have his say.

"You lithten to me!" Thubway Tham said. "If you wath not thtran-gerth in town, you'd know that I am the only man who ith thuppothed to work in the thubway. I am Thubway Tham!"

"Indeed?" Mr. Clackworthy said. "It seems to me that I have heard of you."

"No doubt!" Tham said.

"But I fail to see how you can be of interest to us," Mr. Clackworthy continued. "Possibly you did see James, here, lift a leather. I was just speaking to him concerning it, warning him not to do such a thing again.

It is — er — beneath him."

"A crook ith a crook," Tham said.

"But there are degrees, my dear sir," Mr. Clackworthy said. "My name is Clackworthy. I am from Chicago, here on business, and James could not resist the chance offered him to get some easy money. But I deplore his act. I deplore it deeply."

"Tho you are Clackworthy, are you?" Tham said. "Thomebody wath tellin' me about you jutht a thort time ago. You're the thwindler who goeth around roathtin' dipth and thtickup men, are you?"

"Picking pockets is all right for boys just learning the rudiments of a career of crime," replied Mr. Clackworthy, evading the direct question and wishing not to be rude.

"My goodneth!" Tham said. "And what kind of a crook do you call yourthelf?"

"Do you think for a moment that I would stoop to picking a pocket?" Mr. Clackworthy replied, again evading his question and returning his query with mild sarcasm.

"You couldn't get away with it!" Tham told him hotly.

"Oh, my dear sir! I regret, as I said, that James lifted the leather. I feel quite sure that he will not succumb to such an ignoble temptation again. But I fail to see why you should object."

"It wath in the thubway —" Tham began.

"And how does it happen that you control the pocket picking of the subway?" Mr. Clackworthy inquired. "Have you a concession from the company or the city?"

"It ith underthtood," Tham replied weakly. "There ith thuppothed to be thome honor —"

"Among thieves?" Mr. Clackworthy asked, fully enjoying the discomfiture of Thubway Tham, "My dear sir, you would do better to pursue some other vocation. A man of your age and intelligence should not insist on wasting his life lifting leathers in the detestable subway!"

Mr. Clackworthy had made a mistake. If there was one thing that Thubway Tham admired, it was that same subway that Mr. Clackworthy now scorned. Tham's face went white, and then red.

"They haven't got a thubway in Thicago, have they?" he asked sneeringly. "I thuppothe not! That ith why you make thmall talk about the one we've got here. You're thome man, ain't you? You hate yourthelf — I don't think! Runnin' down the thubway and runnin' down dipth! A dip ith a whole lot cleverer than a common thwindler!"

"Oh, my dear sir!" Mr. Clackworthy said.

"Well, he ith! If a man got your purthe, he could keep it, couldn't he?"

"I'd grant him the privilege," Mr. Clackworthy replied.

"You thimp!" Thubway Tham said, stepping closer to him. "You thilly ath! You thtuck-up Thicago boob! Right under your nothe — and right under the nothe of thith hammered-down, ugly-fathed Thicago thug you've got with you, I've nicked you for your wallet! I did it when thothe two chauffeurth thtarted howlin' at each other in the thtreet a couple of minuteth ago and you and your boob friend looked up to thee what wath the matter! Too clever, are you, to let a dip get in hith work? Thimp!"

"Sir —" Clackworthy began.

"Here ith the wallet — thee?" Thubway Tham held it up, taking it from his coat pocket. "How eathy it wath! Let thith be a lethon."

"You may retain the wallet," said Mr. Clackworthy with becoming dignity. "There is nothing in it except some newspaper clippings and a few counterfeit bills, I always carry that wallet in my hip pocket as bait for dips. I think, my dear sir, that you are badly fooled. You have failed because you lack cleverness. My real funds are in another wallet in the inside pocket of my coat!"

The Early Bird laughed, and Mr. Amos Clackworthy indulged in an ingratiating smile.

"Ith that tho?" Tham asked. "Your real fundth are in another wallet in the inthide pocket of your coat, are they? Huh! Are they? Maybe you'd better look and thee!"

Mr. Clackworthy, in sudden alarm, felt in his pocket, and for a moment he ceased to be his usual calm and dignified self. The inside pocket of his coat was empty!

"You are tho very clever!" said Thubway Tham. "Any dip who getth your roll ith welcome to it, ith he? Very well! Thankth!"

Thubway Tham, chuckling, walked on down the street, and Mr. Amos Clackworthy and The Early Bird let him go.

THUBWAY THAM'S
INTHULT

THE ORCHESTRA ceased, the theater auditorium was darkened suddenly, and the curtain went up on the third act. In his seat in the first row of the second balcony, Thubway Tham bent forward with a great deal of interest and focused his gaze on the stage. His eyes were burning, and his jaws were set rigidly. Tham was angry, had been growing angrier every time a certain actor came upon the stage.

Now and then Thubway Tham attended a theatrical performance as a means of recreation from the arduous work of a pickpocket. Tham did not pretend to be up to the minute on things theatrical and dramatic, and when the time came for him to go to a show, Tham selected the theater he was to honor with his presence by. a certain method he had originated himself.

At the ticket agency he walked up to the counter.

"I want a theat in the thenter of the firtht row of the thecond balcony," he said.

"What theater, man?" asked the man behind the counter.

"I don't care what theater it ith, jutht tho you give me a theat in the thenter of the firtht row of the thecond balcony," Thubway Tham declared.

This time the grinning agent had handed him a ticket that called for admission to see a certain male star in his latest success, "The Under Dog."

Tham had heard the name of the star mentioned a few times and entertained the idea that he was an artist of parts; but beyond that he knew nothing of the professional rank and ability of the man and did not care about it. As to "The Under Dog," Thubway Tham did not know the theme or the author, did not know what the play was about, and was not letting it worry him. Tham had the idea that a good many others have: namely, that a show must be good or it would not be on Broadway

144

or anywhere near it.

Tham had consulted his program, once he had been seated, and he had found nothing except a list of actors' names and the names of the characters they were to portray. The synopsis said that the first act was in the living room of an apartment on Riverside Drive, that the second was the same the following morning, and the third a week later. Thubway Tham could not construct a plot from that, and so he waited for the curtain and left it to the actors.

It developed that "The Under Dog" had nothing to do with canines or bench shows. It dealt with the deadly and eternal triangle, a beautiful woman and two men, one wealthy and firm in the belief that he had power, and the other a sort of weakling. Tham settled himself in his seat and tried to get the worth of the money he had spent for his ticket.

Tham liked the male star very well, but he took an instant aversion to another gentlemanly actor billed as Booth Mansfield Merton. The aversion came into being when Merton spoke his first lines. Tham could not explain it and did not attempt to try. The aversion was not because of Booth Mansfield Merton's work. As an actor, Merton seemed to do very well. Thubway Tham's dislike appeared to be for the man personally, and Tham never had seen him before.

The role Mr. Booth Mansfield Merton played this night did not assist Tham to have a friendly feeling for him, either. Merton spoke certain lines that made Tham gnash his teeth. Thubway Tham took the drama seriously; he forgot that the actors were playing parts, and he formed his opinion of an artist from the lines he spoke. Thubway Tham could not think of a villain as being anything other than a villain, either on the stage or off.

"A man of power should exert that power," Booth Mansfield Merton shouted from the stage. "Every man for himself. Let the under dog fight his own battle. It only weakens him the more to extend him a helping hand. Why should I refuse to declare myself superior when I know that I am?"

Thubway Tham gasped. "Why, the thilly ath," he whispered to himself. "The thwell-headed thimp! Thomebody thould butht him one in the nothe, tho they thould."

Booth Mansfield Merton had a lot of speeches similar to that one, and Thubway Tham's dislike for him slowly but deliberately turned into deep hatred. And then, unknowingly, Booth Mansfield Merton struck home.

"The reputed cleverness of the social parasite, the cunning of the man who lives by his wits, the skill of the pickpocket, for instance — all such things are mythical," the actor vehemently declared. "A superior man can outwit any of them."

"The Thimp," said Tham to himself. "Thuperior, ith he? Oh, the thilly ath! If he ever cometh thouth of Fourteenth Thtreet and I thee him, he wanth to look out. I'll thow him thome cleverneth and thkill, all right!"

Tham left the theater after the performance with the conviction that the ticket agent had robbed him by forcing him to pay good money to be insulted. He rode downtown in the subway, and though there was many a good chance to "lift a leather," Tham did not make an attempt to work. His mind was full of the false philosophy that had come from the lips of Merton.

"Tho a pickpocket ith not clever, hey?" Tham mused. "And thith Booth Manthfield Merton ith a thuperior man who could make the betht dip in the thity look like a deuthe card, ith he? He maketh me thick. I'll teach him to inthult people."

THE FOLLOWING day being Sunday, Thubway Tham arose a little late, spent plenty of time dressing, and walked briskly down the street to the restaurant he always favored for breakfast. It appeared that all the other customers were late for breakfast also. Tham managed to get his usual place at his usual table, but was forced to wait for some time until his order was filled. While waiting he picked up the dramatic section of one of the Sunday morning newspapers, and the first thing he saw was an interview with Booth Mansfield Merton.

The interview was the work of an enterprising press agent, of course, but Thubway Tham knew little concerning the workings of a press agent's mind. Tham did not know that Booth Mansfield Merton never had seen that interview and would be greatly surprised when he read it to find that he had expressed himself so on certain subjects. Tham curled his lips in scorn and read the interview.

It said that Mr. Merton, now playing an important role in the current greatest success of the century, "The Under Dog," was a conscientious artist, and expected, the following season, to appear in a drama that concerned the underworld and its men and women. The play would be something entirely new, Mr. Merton said, and would reveal the denizens of the underworld in a new light.

To be sure that he expressed the proper atmosphere when the play was produced, Mr. Merton — who always was willing to sacrifice comfort to art — was living in the lower end of the city, the article said. He had given up his comfortable apartment on the Drive and had a room far downtown, ate there, walked the streets there when his presence was not demanded at the theater, and was making an exhaustive study of the men and women there, going down into the dark places for the purposes of analysis and comparison.

A few quoted paragraphs from Booth Mansfield Merton followed. He said:

"There has been expressed for some time a certain glamor concerning the so-called underworld that does not exist in reality. The criminals of today are neither courageous nor clever, cunning nor sagacious. Only ignorance is found in the underworld of today — a vicious ignorance that is remarkable."

Thubway Tham felt anger growing within him when he read that paragraph. Tham felt that he was a good "dip," and was rated as such by the police. He was neither ignorant nor vicious. He was a human being, was Tham, and because he picked pockets and belonged to a nefarious profession, it did not follow that he was an unintelligent beast.

"I'd jutht like to meet that thimp," Thubway Tham told himself. "Thtudying the underworld, ith he? I'd thoon give him thomething to thtudy, the ath. He ith a thuperior man, ith he? Thacrifithin' comfort for art, ith he? He'll thacrifith hith bank roll if he cometh around me!"

II.

WITHOUT knowing it, the press agent had let Booth Mansfield Merton in for a lot of trouble. Thubway Tham was not the only gentleman of irregular business who read that interview, and there was an expressed intention on the part of many to seek out Booth Mansfield Merton and "get him good."

But Thubway Tham had a big advantage. He had seen the man at work on the stage and knew him at sight.

"If he only hath a roll on him," Tham mused. "I'll thow the thilly ath a thing or two. Neither cunning nor thagaciouth, am I not? We'll thee."

Determination controlling him, his mind centered upon one object; in a manner of speaking, Thubway Tham deserted his beloved subway for a time and paced the streets, always alert to catch sight of the despised Booth Mansfield Merton. He even watched at the theater one evening and attempted to follow the actor when he left after the performance, but some admirer of Merton's took him to a roof garden for supper, and Tham missed them when they departed.

However, he did not fail to run into Detective Craddock, the particular officer who had sworn to get him "with the goods" one day and send him up the river for a long term. Tham met him as he turned a corner, and stepped back quickly to curl his upper lip in a sneer.

"Tham," Craddock said, "you have been acting peculiarly lately. What seems to be the trouble? Indigestion, or something like that? Going to have a sick spell? Old age, maybe."

"Thay!" cried Tham. "My thtomach ith all right, and I am not goin' to have a thick thpell! And where do you get that old age thtuff, you ath? Bethide you, Craddock, I am ath a thucklin' babe."

"How is the wallet business?" Craddock asked.

"Thay, now —"

"Playing some deep, dark game, aren't you, Thamb? Trying to make me think that you have reformed, to throw me off the track? Something is brewing, Tham. I've had my eye on you carefully the last three days, and you haven't even known it, or cared. And you haven't gone into the subway more than half a dozen times, and when you did you always acted as if there was something preying on your mind. Is your conscience bothering you, Tham?"

"It ith not, but there ith thomething preyin' on my mind, all right. I have been tryin' to figure out," Tham told him, "how it cometh that you thtill draw pay for bein' a fly cop. And it ith thome puthle!"

"Indeed?"

"Quite tho," Tham said. "I thaw in the paper the other day where thome ham actor thaid that crookth had neither courage nor cunnin', cleverneth nor thagacithy. That thimp ought to thtudy offitherth, the tho-called detectiveth in particular. When it cometh down to cleverneth and thagacithy, Craddock, a mule hath nothin' on you."

"Ah well, Tham, old boy, we must each of us have our little, merry jest," Craddock said.

"It ith no merry jetht," Thubway Tham declared. "It ith the truth, only it ith not thurprithin' that you don't recognithe the truth when you thee it."

"All jokes aside, Tham, have you been feeling well lately? I'd hate to have you grow ill and be taken off before I get the chance to run you in and see you put away for a twenty-stretch in stir. That would be what they call the irony of fate, Tham, old-timer."

"Yeth? It ith probable that I thall die of old age before that," Tham remarked. "It ith impothible for a man to hold on forever jutht to pleathe a fly cop."

"You'll not be much older when it happens, Tham."

"No?"

"No! You'll make that little slip one of these days, and then it'll be up the river for you."

"If I did make that little thlip, you wouldn't be able to thee it," Tham complained. "You couldn't thee anything right under your long nothe."

Tham whirled around and deliberately left Craddock, going toward Union Square. Thubway Tham was in a rare bad humor. He had failed so far to locate Booth Mansfield Merton, and Craddock's pestering ways annoyed him exceedingly.

And then he saw the actor!

Booth Mansfield Merton was walking languidly along the street, his nose in the air and a far-away look in his eyes. He swung his stick as if to clear a path through the rabble. He was smoking a cigarette, in a holder.

"The ath!" Tham said.

And then he began to shadow and study Booth Mansfield Merton. Tham had a scheme in mind. He wanted to get Merton's wallet when it was well filled. He wanted Merton to know that there was one crook who had cleverness and sagacity enough to "lift a leather" even from such a wise individual as Booth Mansfield Merton.

Merton evidently was taking the air. Now and then he paused to look into a show window before a shop, but for the greater part he looked at the men and women who passed as if studying them. Tham trailed him faithfully.

"Firtht, I mutht be thure that he hath a roll," Tham told himself. "And then I mutht find out where he liveth and when he goeth uptown to the theater. And then I jutht want to catch the thimp in the thubway onthe. That ith all — jutht onthe!"

For Tham did not think of robbing Booth Mansfield Merton any place except in the subway. Tham rarely worked in the open street; he had made the subway his specialty for years. And so he trailed Merton down one street and up another, to a restaurant where Merton ate cakes and drank coffee, to a cigar store where the actor purchased a pack of cigarettes.

"The ath thmoketh cheap cigaretteth in an ecthpenthive holder," Tham observed. "If he ith broke, it will be bad luck. But I gueth he ith not."

It was a matinee day, and, after a time, Merton turned and walked northward, and when he was far enough he crossed to the Avenue and caught a bus. Tham got on the same one, and they rode to the theatrical district, where Merton went in at the stage entrance of the theater where he worked.

Tham loafed around Times Square until time for the afternoon performance to be at an end, and then watched the stage entrance carefully. He saw Merton emerge, in company with another actor. They went to an inexpensive café and ordered a meal. Then Tham realized that he had been wasting time. Since this was a matinee day, it was more than likely that Merton would not return downtown until after the evening performance.

However, Tham shadowed his man until he returned to the theater to make up, and then he went to a picture show, careful to get back to the stage entrance by the time Merton was leaving for the night. This time, Merton made straight for the subway entrance nearest the theater, and Tham, exulting, followed.

When Booth Mansfield Merton entered the car, Thubway Tham was less than six feet behind him. The car was not crowded, and Merton sat down. He engaged in conversation with an acquaintance, and Tham could not make an attempt to get his purse. But when Merton left the subway, Tham followed carefully, and he located the actor's lodgings.

Tham hurried to his own room and turned in. He was up two hours earlier than usual the following morning, bolted his breakfast at the little restaurant, and then went to the place where Merton lived. For several hours Thubway Tham remained in the vicinity, moving now and then to keep from attracting attention, waiting for Merton to leave his room.

"The ath mutht thleep all day," Tham confided to himself. "He ith a lathy thcoundrel!"

Then Merton came out. Once more he walked slowly up the street, swinging his stick as if to clear a path through the rabble, looking over the heads of the men and women he met. Tham followed him, watched him eat a frugal breakfast, and followed him on up the street. Booth Mansfield Merton took a bus northward again, at which Thubway Tham gnashed his teeth.

"Nobody with clath utheth a buth," Tham declared, "when there ith the thubway handy."

Uptown, Merton strolled through the streets of the theatrical district, greeting other thespians and talking shop, and Thubway Tham continued to trail him. And again he met Detective Craddock.

"Well, Tham, what are you doing up here?" Craddock demanded.

"I might athk you the thame quethtion," Tham replied. "Ith thith your beat now?"

"I just happen to be here momentarily, Tham."

"Tho do I."

"Changing your tactics, are you ? Deserting the subway and going after the street crowds now?"

"Thay! Are you accuthin' me of anything?" Tham demanded. "Don't you thuppothe a man wanth to thee another part of town onthe in a while?"

"Take care of your fingers, old boy, or they'll be getting you into trouble," Craddock told him. "I'm liable to be in your vicinity any time, remember."

"Ith that tho? You needn't trouble to be in my vithinity ath far ath I am contherned," said Tham. "There are timeth when I like freth air."

"That's almost insulting, Tham."

"It would be a pity if I inthulted you," Tham said. "But I won't. It can't be done!"

Craddock walked on, for he was watching a suspect, and Tham saw that Booth Mansfield Merton was in conversation with another man near the corner. Then they separated, and Merton went on down the street. Tham followed.

The actor entered a corner cigar store, and Tham watched through the door and saw a thing that startled him. Mr. Merton purchased a package of cigarettes, and when he came to pay for them he took from the side pocket of his coat a roll of bills about four inches in diameter. He peeled off a bill and thrust the roll back, gathered his change and put it into a pocket of his waistcoat, lighted a cigarette, twirled his stick, and went out upon the street again.

Thubway Tham gasped as he followed.

"Oh, man," he said to himself. "If I can get that roll of billth I can die happy. Thagacithy and cunnin', huh? Neither cleverneth nor courage! Oh, man!"

Tham had heard that good actors drew down fabulous salaries and were likely to carry the cash around with them. So he decided that the roll of Booth Mansfield Merton would be worth appropriating. Aside from that, Tham wanted to get the roll as a matter of revenge against the man who sa'id such high and lofty things against the under dogs at every performance.

But it did not seem that he would have his chance. Merton continued to parade the rialto, chatting with an acquaintance now amd then, and Tham saw him flash the big roll half a dozen times Thubway Tham was almost frantic now. He could think of nothing except the roll of bills. He ignored the rush hour, and all chances to "lift a leather." For the time being, Thubway Tham had one big important job in sight, and nothing could decoy him from it.

III.

"I MUTHT get that roll," Tham told himself, for the hundredth time since he had seen it first. "Live downtown to thtu the animalth, will he? Huh! Viciouth ignorance, hey?"

Late in the afternoon Booth Mansfield Merton parted from another acquaintance and started for a subway entrance. Thubway Tham followed like a bloodhound on a trail. Tham felt that his time had come at last. He had seen Merton return that roll to the side pocket of his coat, and he knew it still. was there. And Merton was going into the subway!

Merton caught a downtown express, and Thubway Tham squeezed into the car immediately behind him. This time the actor was forced to stand, and Tham bored his way through the crowd in an effort to get by his prospective victim's side.

Tham glanced around the car, slowly, carefully, and saw nobody he knew. He would use his usual method, Tham decided. He would wait until the train pulled into a station, and just before it pulled out again he would get Merton's roll, dart through the door, and hurry to the street above.

Tham did not deem the moment propitious when the first station was reached. An elderly woman, half bewildered, was hurrying to leave the train and attracting the attention of everybody in the car toward the spot where Tham and Merton stood.

But a station more or less made little difference to Thubway Tham. It was the outcome that interested him. He wanted to get that roll, and do it successfully, and he cared nothing for time.

The train dashed on. Tham decided that the next station would be the proper place. He edged forward until he was brushing against Booth Mansfield Merton, and placed himself in such a position that he could slip his hand into Merton's pocket and get the roll in the proper manner. As a last precaution, he glanced around the car again.

And he caught sight of Detective Craddock, who had been watching him carefully, and who now allowed an expression of annoyance to cross his countenance. Tham turned away and grinned. Craddock almost had caught him; it was a fortunate thing that he looked around at the last moment. Craddock, who knew pickpockes, had guessed that Tham had picked Merton for a victim.

Tham left the car when the train stopped, left it slowly and without brushing against Merton again. Craddock followed him to the street.

"Well, old-timer," Craddock said, "I almost had you that time."

"Thir?"

"Don't come any of that stuff on me, now. You had your little victim picked, all right, and you hadn't seen me at first. If you hadn't happened to look around when you did, you'd have pulled off a stunt, and then I'd nabbed you with the goods. But I'll get you yet, Tham."

"Are you an utter ath?" Tham demanded. "What are you talkin' about, Craddock? I wath intendin' to do nothin' of the thort. I wath jutht gettin' ready to get off."

"I know what you were getting ready to do," Craddock said with a sneer.

He glared at Tham and went on down the street. And Thubway Tham, angry and chagrined, went to a restaurant for his evening meal, and then went back uptown again, intending to be at the stage door when Merton left the theater that night.

"I'll get that roll of hith if it taketh me a dothen yearth," Tham declared to himself. "When it cometh to bein' perthithtent, I am a medal winner."

Tham arrived uptown again about nine o'clock that night, and walked around Times Square, glancing at his watch now and then. He would see Booth Mansfield Merton come from the theater, he would trail him well, and if Merton traveled downtown in the subway, he would get that roll of bills, providing Merton still had it. Tham was half afraid that the roll would be missing.

Everything depended upon it, Tham told himself. He wanted to feel that he had squared matters with Merton. And his chase had caused him to lose several days and turn aside chances for lucrative work. Tham needed the roll as much as he wanted his revenge.

Ten o'clock came, and Tham, having purchased some cigarettes, turned to light one. Looking over his cupped hands, he beheld Detective Craddock across the street, watching him. Tham pretended not to see. Growling low in his throat, he started down the street.

But Craddock was not to be thrown off the trail that easily. He hurried forward and caught up with Tham.

"All jokes aside, what are you camping in this section of our fair city for?" Craddock demanded. "You're up to something, and I'm going to stop it."

"Yeth?"

"Yes."

"Well, my goodneth, ain't a man got a right to look at the bright lighth?"

"If that is all he does," Craddock insinuated.

"Thuppothe you wait until I do thomething elthe," said Tham.

"I'll just do that little thing," the detective said. "Go your way, old-timer; I'll be right at your heels."

Tham was almost in a panic. He knew from observation that Booth Mansfield Merton would come from that stage door at about eleven o'clock, and it was a little past ten now. If he did not lose Craddock before that time, he would not dare seek to obtain possession of Merton's roll of bills.

He darted into the subway entrance at Times Square, crossed through and emerged on the other side, and found that the grinning Craddock was only a few paces behind him. He walked slowly up Broadway and into the midst of a throng before a motion-picture palace, but he could not lose Craddock as he had done many times before. Craddock had determined not to be evaded this night.

Thubway Tham attempted every trick he knew, but to no avail. The detective hung on like a leech, and whenever Tham turned to glance at him, Craddock grinned. Tham looked at his watch finally; it was fifteen minutes of eleven.

Once more he walked slowly Jown Broadway, ignoring Craddock, not trying to lose himself in a crowd, acting as if he had given up hope of dodging the detective, and was preparing to return to his room far down-town.

But Craddock was not to be fooled, and did not relax his vigilance. He followed closely, lighting cigar after cigar, as he did always when he was shadowing and it was possible.

So Tham came to a stop on the corner nearest the stage entrance of the theater where Booth Mansfield Merton was playing. There he stood at the curb and smoked, and watched the stage entrance from the corner of his eye.

"Dodging doesn't go tonight, Tham," Craddock said.

"Don't pethter me," Tham retorted. "If you want to talk to thome-body, go and do it."

"I can watch you as easily if I don't talk," said Craddock.

"Watch," Tham said. "Watch, you thilly ath! And while you are watchin' and pethterin' me, thome crook probably ith gettin' all the diamondth and walletth in the theater crowd. Watch, you thimp!"

"Oh, I'm watching, Tham."

"And a lot of good it will do you," Tham said. "I'm goin' down and thee the commithioner about thith! It ith a fine day when a man and a thitithen cannot walk around the thtreeth and take the air without bein' pethtered."

"The commissioner probably will be glad to see you, Tham. He might want to know how you get money to pay room rent and buy eats."

"Yeth?"

"Yes. He has a way of asking about such things. Better think twice before visiting the commissioner, Tham."

"Then you let me alone," Tham said. "I ain't done anything, have I?"

"No, and it is my intention to see that you don't," Craddock declared.

Tham shrugged his shoulders and turned his back. And so he faced the stage entrance again — and he saw Booth Mansfield Merton come out with another actor and walk slowly toward the corner.

Here was the chance, Tham knew, providing Merton still had the big roll of bills. And because of Craddock, it appeared that Tham's persistance was going to come to naught. Outwardly, Tham looked calm, but he was not.

He turned away and walked slowly toward the subway entrance, following Merton at a distance,. He tossed away his cigarette and went down the stairs half a dozen steps behind the thespian. Craddock was at his heels.

They waited on the platform for a time, and then a train roared in. Tham followed Merton aboard, but not too closely, and Craddock, still grinning, followed Tham. Merton had to stand near the door, and Tham stood beside him.

Tham was not certain that the roll of bills remained in Merton's pocket. He wanted to find out, and, if it did, he wanted to get it. And here was Detective Craddock, who had sworn to "get him with the goods," standing at his elbow.

Tham decided, in that instant, that the opportunity should not be wasted. He had persisted in following Booth Mansfield Merton, and he felt that he was entitled to some sort of reward. It was dangerous to attempt anything in Craddock's presence, but Tham was angry enough to run the risk. He would not have done it had he not been asgry.

He turned deliberately and faced Craddock, but still pressed against the actor.

"I hope that you are thatithfied," he said to Craddock, in a low tone. "You have thpoiled my evenin'."

"Oh, I certainly regret that, Tham," Craddock said, with a wealth of sarcasm.

"But one thing ith thertain. You have to follow me 'way downtown, and then go 'way out to the Bronx to get home. That ith thomething."

"I don't mind a little thing like that, Tham."

"How much longer are you goin' to pethter me?"

"I merely intend to see you safely home, my dear boy."

Tham grunted and looked past Craddock at the others in the car. His left hand had been pressing against Merton, exploring. Tham knew, now, that the roll of bills was still in Merton's pocket.

Tham did not like to work blind, that is with his hand behind his back and not knowing who might be looking, but he felt that he would have to do it now. This was an opportunity he could not reject, Craddock or no Craddock.

He continued talking to the detective, and watching the stations. And then, as the train rolled into another, Tham acted. His hand darted into the actor's pocket — and Tham had the roll of bills.

"Here ith where I get off," he told Craddock.

"I'm getting off at the same station, Tham."

"Do ath you pleathe, you ath!"

The train stopped, and Tham got off and went slowly along the platform and up to the street, expecting every instant to hear a cry from Booth Mansfield Merton. But no cry came, and the train rushed on.

"I thuppothe you are goin' to go right along home with me?" Tham asked, gneeringly.

"It isn't necessary now, Tham, old boy. I know you seldom work except in the subway. And now that you are out of it and within three blocks of home, and the hour is late, I imagine I can let you go on your way alone."

"Thankth."

"I saw you sizing up that bird who stood right next to you," Craddock said.

"Tho?"

"And you didn't miss anything by not getting his wallet. I know that chap."

"Yeth?"

"Yes," said Craddock. "He's an actor — nice fellow, too. But he certainly has been down on his luck the past three seasons. He's just about broken — owes all sorts of people. There was an article in the paper about him the other morning — press-agent stuff."

"Tho?"

"Yes. It said he was living down here to study criminals and human beings of the lower order, because he was going to do a play along those lines next year."

"Well, what about it?" Tham asked.

"He's trying to pay his debts. He's living down here because he can't afford an apartment up on the Drive. It's all bunk about getting proper atmosphere. He's got a cheap room and eats in cheap restaurants. Just press-agent bunk. So, you see, if you had taken a crack at his wallet, you'd probably have come out loser."

"Tho?" Tham said. "Well, that's all right, then. Broke, ith he? Tho! Ath if I cared!"

Tham walked on down the street, and Craddock allowed him to go. As soon as his back was turned, Tham began to grin. Craddock knew it all, did he? Merton was broke and trying to live cheap, was he? He rented a poor room and ate in cheap restaurants and pretended it was for art, did he? Well, Tham happened to know that he had coin — or that he had had it. Right now Tham had a roll of bills —

"And I got 'em right under that thilly Craddock'th nothe," he told himself. "I'll bet it ith thome roll, too!"

SAFE IN his room, Thubway Tham pulled the roll of bills from his pocket and sat down on the side of the bed to count the currency. It certainly was an imposing roll. On the outside was a ten-dollar bill. Tham peeled back the corner, and saw beneath it a five-dollar bill; then he peeled back the corner of that.

Ten seconds later, Thubway Tham was standing in the middle of the room, tearing his hair and vowing that there should come a day when Booth Mansfield Merton should pay. Save for these two negotiable bills, the roll was stage money — merely a "flash" roll!

Detective Craddock had been right. Merton was "broke," but trying to keep up appearances, pretending prosperity where there was none.

"And I perthithted," said Tham mournfully. "I jutht hung on to that man! Perthithtenthe getth a man nothin' in a cathe like thith. It ith jutht a wathte of time."

He looked down at the heap of stage money on the floor at his feet and then grinned. "It ith a good joke," he said. "I'll jutht keep that thtuff and flath it mythelf. And anyway, I gueth that fellow will know enough netht time not to inthult people as he pleatheth."